AMONG THE MAD PEOPLE

AMONG THE MAD PEOPLE

SAPNA SHRIHARSHA

PARTRIDGE

To order additional copies of this book, contact
Partridge India
000 800 10062 62
orders.india@partridgepublishing.com

www.partridgepublishing.com/india

Acknowledgements

M Y FOREMOST AND HUMBLE THANKS, to my editor and Cousin, Sushruth G. Thanks a lot for reading my manuscript and giving me fresh ideas.

I thank my husband, Dr Shriharsha, for his love and patience. I also thank my adorable and naughty children Srushti and Samarth, without their love, I am incomplete.

I thank my family for their support and encouragement.

I owe my gratitude to all my friends, in particular Navya Narayanan for being with me and encouraging me while writing this novel.

My humble thanks to my publisher for their services and their passion.

The unknown secrets of a man will be unknown forever,
unless the man reveals by himself.

No one can peep, deep inside the mind and look into
the bright and dark shades of life, unless, one gives the way.

Chapter 1

THE CHILD BELLOWED, FOR WHAT the man did to the child was something atrocious.

"No!,,,,,,,, please stop it,,, No,,,,,,,,,,,," the child cried, but no one helped him.

Tom awoke perspiring in trepidation and he could feel his heart bouncing inside his chest. The night mare often haunted him and he dreaded it. He sat berserk facing the white wall in front of him. He was still gasping for breath.

"I cannot tolerate this anymore!" he was fretting.

He then noticed his surroundings. The neat white walls, windows with draped curtains, an intravenous line next to him, medicines, fruits and flowers, everything conveyed that he was in a hospital.

He tried recollecting his recent past. "What happened? How did I come here?"

Tom felt a sudden intense throbbing headache. He was dazed and confused about what had happened. He sat thinking, when suddenly his left hand slapped him and pulled away the intravenous line on his right hand. The needle was out and it started bleeding.

Tom starred in disorientation as his left hand behaved freakily. It was totally uncontrollable. "What the hell!!!" he yelled

Outside, in nurses' station, a few were running around with trays in their hands and few had a quick gossip with each other.

"Did you see the new Doc? Oh my god! He is so handsome,,"

"Dr Siddanth, right? Awe! he really is. Handsome psychiatrist, I must say"

"Yes, I wish I get posting in his OPD"

"Or you might get admitted under him for false state of depression!" she giggled.

"Not a bad idea, better to be near him than away"

"I envy that Alice! She was fortunate enough to be posted with him" the nurse sniffed.

'And the good news is,,, he is still single!! Oh! I pray that I end up getting married to him' she closed her eyes in small prayer.

"What are you praying for? The doc! Stop day dreaming,,, he,,,," she stopped when the red button buzzed in nurse station. It was from room 204.

"204? Did the patient regain his conscious? I have to inform the Doc. But, let me check out first"

She hurried towards the room. As she opened the door, she stood shocked for a moment. Blood was dripping from his hand and it had soaked the bed.

She quickly ran back to the nurse station. "204 patient! His IV line is out and he is bleeding. I pray that he doesn't become unconscious again. Oh, the doctor will fire me for negligence."

"Hey don't get tensed, just give him compression bandage and re prick on his other hand. I will inform the doc. You carry on,,"

She hurried with a tray in her hand.

"Don't worry Tom. Please,, relax. I will handle it" she took a sterile white pad and then rubbed the blood. She put white pads on the wound and gave a compression pressure. She waited for three minutes and took of the pads. The blood had stopped oozing. She put a bandage.

"Now,,,,,, I have to search for a new vein. It's just a prick" she tried pacifying him and took his left hand to screen.

"Tighten your fist, Tom…" she found a vein, cleansed the site with sterile pad and was about to prick.

Tom instantly withdrew his hand and slapped her.

"Tom! How dare you!" she looked at him furiously.

"Oh,, I am sorry nurse, I didn't mean to" he searched for words to substantiate. "I am, really sorry. I have a bad headache and my left hand just won't listen to me"

"Don't be silly. Show me your hand for IV line or I will walk off" she gave a grimace of distaste.

She screened his left hand for veins but instantly he withdrew his hand and groped her breast.

The nurse slapped him hard and snapped. "This is ridiculous! You are just a bloody pervert and nothing else. I will inform the authorities"

She ran to the nurse station and started weeping.

"What happened why are you crying?"

"He is a bloody bastard! I was trying to find new veins and he slapped me! Can you believe that?"

"What? You should have slapped him back"

"I warned him and continued my work. But that idiot groped my breast!"

"Oh my god! He squeezed your breast! Left or right? Was he rough? Was he gentle?" she giggled.

"Shut up! If I had stayed there even an extra minute, I think he would have raped me"

"I think he is a pervert or may be a rapist too. We didn't find any identity cards of him when he was brought here. We better inform the police. They may know him better. But before, we have to inform our medical superintendent first"

The nurses hurried towards the medical superintendent room.

"Sir, there is a problem"

The superintendent cocked his brow and snapped. "You nurses,,,, always have problems. You don't want posting in casualties, ICU s and internal fights among yourselves. Don't irritate me. Meet your matron and discuss."

"Sir, this is regarding a patient" and she slowly explained him everything in detail.

The doctor frowned "ok,,,, I will look into the matter. Who is the doctor in charge of that patient?"

"Dr Philip"

"I will discuss with him. Now get back to work"

The medical superintendent dialed a number in the intercom. "Dr Philip, I have to discuss something with you. Can you come to my chamber?"

The doctor arrived quickly.

"Ah Dr Philip, please sit down. I just received a complaint"

Dr Philip looked at him confused "Complaint on me?"

The medical superintendent laughed "ah! Not on you. The nurse complained about your patient"

"My patient?"

"Yes room 204,, patient name is Tom. The nurse complained that Tom is a pervert; he slapped her and then groped her breast! They fear that he may be a rapist. What is his case? How did he land up here?"

Dr Philip was surprised "Sir, he had an accident last night. He had collided with a car. Some villagers brought him. He was unconscious. I examined him and subjected him to all investigations. He had subdural hematoma. He was stabilized and was shifted to the ward. A few minutes back, I received a call from nurse station. A nurse said that he regained his conscious,. I was about to see him, but you called me, so I had to come here."

"He didn't have any identity cards when he landed here. Then how do you know that, his name is Tom?"

"He has a tattoo on his back which reads TOM"

"Talk to him. Try getting his details. Then we shall decide on further action. We may have to inform the police too. An unidentified stranger is admitted in our hospital. They may help us"

"Sure sir" Dr Philip left the room.

Dr Philip walked towards the room 204. He opened the door and slowly entered.

Tom looked at him with a blank expression.

"Good morning Tom. I am Dr Philip. So, how are you feeling?"

"I have a severe headache" Tom clutched his head.

"Do not worry. You will be fine. Can you remember what happened last night?"

"No,, I don't"

"You met with an accident and you had a head injury. To be precise, you had a subdural hematoma"

"Hematoma?" Tom looked at the doctor perplexed.

"Blood clot in brain" Dr Philip explained. "Can you tell who you are and give your family details? We shall contact them immediately.

"Family?"

"Yes,,, your family members. Tell us their names and give phone number"

"I am not able to remember now. I am having headache" he groaned in pain.

"Ok take rest. You may be having retrograde amnesia. With time you will recover. I have to ask you something. Why did you slap the nurse and squeezed her breast?"

"I am sorry for that doc. But I didn't do it. It was my left hand"

"What do you mean?"

"I mean, my left hand does things on its own. It doesn't obey me"

"What are you saying Tom? Stop feigning!"

"I am speaking the truth. My left hand doesn't obey me. I think it is possessed by some devil"

"Enough Tom, I don't want to hear anymore nonsense. The nurses are afraid to come to your room. They think you are a pervert. I will arrange a brother to take care of you. You can ask his help, as long as you are here"

Tom yelled "I am not a pervert! It's my left hand" he clutched his head.

Dr Philip consoled him and added some medicines.

"You need rest. If you remember any of your family members or friends, quickly tell us. See you tomorrow"

Dr Philip gave some instructions to the male nurse and left.

Tom dawdled towards the bathroom and splashed cold water on his face. He peered into the mirror. The mirror was mocking him. It showed a young man of twenties, whose head, beard and mustache, completely shaved. His face was gaunt and sunken and he looked withered.

He removed his clothes and looked at his body. He stood stunned for a second. He looked emaciated and he craved for food.

Then, there was retribution in his eyes. Something inside him said

KILL THE BASTARDS,,,,, DON'T LEAVE THEM.

He wondered who was ordering him and why? Then the surreal memories came in and flooded his brain. He was grief stricken and his heart was shattered in pieces. The agony was unbearable.

Abruptly his left hand slapped him. GO KILL the voice commanded. Tom looked puzzled for a second. He slouched and shrieked.

STOP IT YOU MORON, DON'T CRY LIKE A FOOL. DO AS I SAY, his left hand slapped him again.

The male nurse entered the room. Tom was not in his bed. He heard water flowing in the bathroom.

"Tom, do you need help?" Alex asked.

"Yes, can you come inside?"

Alex opened the door and went inside the bathroom.

It was late in the night. The nurses had dinner and gossiped.

"Where is Alex? I have not seen him since evening."

"Tom and Alex must be having nice time in the room. I mean gay sex!" the nurses giggled.

"Ok,,,,, let's check on them"

They slowly opened the door and peeped. They were baffled for a moment.

The room was empty.

"Where the hell did they vanish?"

One of the nurses ran towards the bathroom. It was locked from outside. She opened it and screamed. The others arrived to check.

Alex was lying in the bathroom. His mouth was filled with tissue papers and was plastered. He was manacled with bandages.

The nurses quickly released the knots and freed him.

"What happened? Where is Tom?"

Alex slowly uttered "Tom escaped"

"Escaped?"

"This is an emergency. We have to quickly inform the authorities."

They ran to nurse station and dialed the intercom.

The medical superintendent was on his night patrol, checking the ICU and other wards. His mobile phone buzzed in his pockets.

He picked up the phone.

"Sir! An emergency! Room 204, patient Tom has escaped." The nurse was panting.

"What? I will be there in a minute" He hurried and saw Alex in nurse station.

"What happened?"

Alex narrated "Tom was in the bathroom. I asked him, whether he needed help. He said yes, and I went inside. He quickly hit me with a bucket, stuffed some tissue papers in my mouth. I tried to refrain, but in vain. He then tied me up with bandages. He put on my dress and identity card and escaped."

The medical superintendent was shocked and repented that he didn't take much care. What if he was really a criminal? "I should have informed the police earlier. We shall check the cctv footage and then inform the police." The medical superintendent hurried towards the computer room.

Chapter 2

A FEW YEARS AGO, IN A medical college, a new batch of students had entered the campus pursuing to become great doctors to treat the world.

It was the first day in the college and there was amalgamation of students from various walks of life, from various regions of the country with one common goal in their minds, to become doctors and serve the society. Fear and anxiety had crept in the novice minds of newcomers.

An orientation day was organized to welcome them, to nurture their dreams and deliver words of wisdom. The day began with a welcome, invocation, blessings from the almighty, address by the Dean of the college.

"A very hearty congratulations for entering this prestigious institution. You have chosen a Nobel profession of service and sacrifice. I am glad about your decision. Things have changed so much in medical profession. I still remember the day when I stood just like one of you facing the Dean of my time. The technology has improved a lot,,,, now you are witnessing the virtual world and can navigate databases"

As the Dean finished his speech the students were in high spirits and they felt they had made a right decision.

The students were then taken throughout the campus and were shown various departments, hospitals and wards. Then they dispersed for lunch.

The second day, the students visited the anatomy department. The head of the department welcomed them and took them to the dissection hall. Some students were apprehensive entering the dissection hall. Inside the hall, they saw a board with words written boldly.

Dissection is an act of introspection. By unwrapping the layers of the donors gift, participants uncover hidden layers of themselves.

Within few seconds, formalin vapors engulfed them and made them close their nostrils.

"You have to get used to this formalin vapors. From now on, cadaver is your god! It will teach you everything hidden in it. You are lucky in this modern era where you have readymade corpses on your table. Think of olden days, the courage of olden men who had to take out corpses from fresh grave sites in middle of the night. They were called body snatchers or resurrectionists. According to history, people started murdering to provide corpses to medical schools. It was then the anatomy act came in 1832." The professor was speaking with a firm, professional cadence.

After hearing the professor s lecture, the students were divided in groups. Each group had twelve members and one instructor.

The students stood around their allotted tables. They looked at the cadavers which were placed before them. A look of awe and fear was seen in their faces. They were embarking on the world of medicine in a salient way for the first time.

Instructions were given and a demonstration was showed. "The first cut is frightening". The professor could here whispers.

After few days the dissection was less intimidating and had become more instinctive. The students kept names for their cadavers. A few dead bodies were of old men and women and few were of young teenagers.

"This lady looks cold and scary. How did she die?" One student said aloud.

"May be her boyfriend murdered her" another student giggled.

The dissection classes were fun with all those cadavers and some naughty jokes among students as they dissected private parts of cadavers.

As a customary, a fresher s day was organized. It was a welcome party for the newcomers to motivate them and make them feel at home. The seniors loved it as it was an opportunity to break the ice, interact with the juniors as well rag them. Though an anti-ragging committee was established, a minor amount of ragging had continued.

A beautiful entertaining cultural extravaganza comprising of dances, melody songs and games were well organized.

Several games were organized and the most important game was of 'Truth or dare'. The player had to choose between answering a question truthfully or perform a dare. It was compulsory for all the fresher's to participate.

Some chose truth and some chose dare. They enjoyed and cackled.

Pranav felt uneasy and wanted to escape but his name was called.

"What you want? Truth or dare?"

"Me,,,,,,,,,,, dare" Pranav said timidly.

"Good! Boys should always dare. The task is to stand on an ice block for a minimum of fifteen minutes and at the end, kneel on the same ice and give a rose to a girl. Pick up a chit. It has the name of the girl."

Standing on an ice block was not a problem for Pranav, but to propose a girl would be the last thing he would do. He hated women.

"I can stand on ice as long as you want me to, but I don't want to propose"

"Shut up. You do not have choice. Do as we say" the senior snarled.

Pranav had to oblige and he picked up the paper with alienation. The senior snatched the paper and opened it. "Good! You have obeyed" he said despicably.

"Prisha! Come forward" the senior called out.

The students looked at each other. A girl emerged slowly from the crowd. She wore a pink dress and her long hair glittered in sun. She was beautiful. All eyes focused on her and the crowd cheered as she stepped forward.

For the first time in his life, he was mesmerized by a beauty. But his ego, arrogance and detestation against women surpassed other feelings. He felt all beautiful women are whores.

He stared at her in revulsion.

Prisha neared him.

"Come on boy! Stand on the ice block"

Pranav removed his shoes and stood bare foot on the ice block. The coldness slowly succumbed his feet. He started feeling numb.

Pranav stood still and looked on in abomination. The students tried boosting him up.

His toes started turning red. He wanted to quit.

But he had asked for a dare, he would be mocked if he fails.

It was the last two minutes, he really wanted to fall apart, but he continued.

He heard a huge applause as he completed the fifteen minutes challenge.

At last,, he had won. He felt triumphed.

"Good buddy! You are commendable. Now do the next task. Propose her." The organizer told him.

Happiness doesn't last long and it often vanishes before we realize it. He didn't want to propose. It was against his will and ego. He still heard the crowd cheering his name.

Prisha walked near him. "Wow! You were good. I thought you would quit the ice block in five minutes. But, you stood still, like a rock. Great! Congratulations"

Pranav didn't know what to say, he stared at her with a blank face. Then he slowly pulled a rose off his pocket and gave her.

"Hello boy! Not just giving the rose, propose her. It's just a game. Be sportive" his friends said loudly.

"I love you" he whispered.

"Sorry pal, we are not able to hear you. Louder!"

"I love you!" Pranav shouted.

Prisha grinned and took the rose. Before she could react, Pranav pulled off the crowd and walked away. Prisha was surprised "ok forget it!" she said and walked back.

The following day in the anatomy dissection hall, he found his table mates giggling. Prisha was in his table and as a batch they had to dissect the body together. He couldn't face her, but being in the same table, he had to.

Her presence annoyed him. While dissecting together, her hands touched his. Pranav hated it and he couldn't concentrate.

Prisha noticed the indifference and she tried avoiding him. The classes went on and an internal assessment was announced. The students thronged on the textbooks and tried studying hard.

Pranav couldn't concentrate on his books and he failed in the exam. Prisha was topper of the class. She was made the table leader.

The professor held a meeting with all the candidates who had failed in their internal assessments. "I can understand your depression. It's a whole new world and terminologies. It may seem difficult,,,,, but,,, not impossible. You need to work hard to fulfill your dreams. You can approach us whenever you have doubts and you cannot understand the subject. You can even take help from your peers. Pranav,,,, you can ask guidance from Prisha. She has topped the class. You both are in the same table. You can converse with each other and solicit her help. Remember, your only aim is to learn and become a good doctor."

"Taking help from her! No way! I would rather fail." Pranav thought in his mind.

Six months had passed and Pranav had no idea of what he was doing.

"I want to meet your parents. Tell them to meet me" the professor said imperiously.

"But,,, why sir?"

"Your grades are getting worse my boy. I need to tell them that you are not able to cope up"

"Sir, I will try improving myself,,, please,, give me a chance" he pleaded.

The professor nodded hesitantly "Study hard my boy."

Pranav walked off, thinking what to do next. That afternoon he stood beside Prisha and observed how she dissected.

"I need your help in studies" Pranav whispered in her ears.

She was startled for a second. She couldn't believe how an arrogant, egoistic jackass was asking for her help.

"Excuse me, can you repeat what you said?" she cocked her brow.

Pranav was breaking the ice. "I need your help in my studies"

"Six months have passed and this is the first time, you are talking to me. It's startling!"

"Just three months left for final exam. I need to pass" he blabbered.

"I agree. But, why me? I mean, you could have asked anybody else? Your friends"

"You are the topper of the class and I have seen how good you are. I felt you would be better"

"Thanks for the compliment. I still can't digest what you said. But, I will help you. You have to promise me that, you will follow my instructions and not question me. If that is ok, I will finalize the deal" she grinned.

"I will do as you say. It's a deal" there was a faint smirk in his face.

Prisha gave him assignments, small tests, frequently questioned him about subject. Pranav started showing improvement.

Several questions troubled his mind "why did I approach her? Why am I enticed by her beauty? Why does her charming attitude attract me?"

They met in library every day and discussed. The final internal assessment was over and to his surprise he had passed.

"I am truly grateful to you. I can't believe that I have passed. You have helped me a lot. Thank you so much"

"I am happy too. I knew I have good teaching skills. We need to celebrate this. So when are you giving party? Prisha smiled

"Anytime, anywhere! It's your wish" he grinned.

"How about this weekend, in café de Loto?"

"Ya sure"

Pranav was in hostel. He lay on bed brooding over his emotions. He stared at the ceiling and contemplated over his feelings. He hated women and he had pledged, not to fall in love. But, now, things had changed. He was slowly falling for her. It was perplexing.

He closed his eyes and saw her sparkling eyes, haughty laughter and long silky hair. "Why do I like her? I can t and I should not." Deep down in his heart he was craving for her. The edifice had crumbled and his burning ego had melted.

He saw the watch. It was 4 in the evening. "I have to meet her. No, actually I am having a date with her. I can't believe myself. How can I change so much?"

He stood in front of his cupboard, thinking which shirt to wear, Red? No,,,,, it was not valentine s day and she may laugh seeing me in bright red shirt! Yellow,,,,,,, that would be too odd! After searching for a while, he finally settled on a brown shirt. Blue jeans would be fine, he thought.

He put on the new perfume he had brought the previous day. He looked into the mirror. Not bad,, he thought.

He drove his bike in apprehension. He reached the café.

He slowly entered and was surprised to see the crowd. The groups were having fun in their own party and the couples cajoled each other, lost in revere. He searched for her.

Finally her beaming face caught her. She was laughing with someone.

Pranav was shattered to see her with another guy. He felt insulted "how could she do this?" he vexed. He took back his steps and wanted to leave when suddenly she called him.

"Come!" she called out.

He walked towards her in hesitation.

"Hi Pranav,, meet Siddanth, my friend" Prisha introduced each other.

"Hello Pranav. I have seen you in hostel but didn't have an opportunity to talk to you"

"You are in my hostel?" Pranav inquired.

"I am in third year. I stay in the same hostel in 4th floor" Siddanth grinned.

Are they a couple? He couldn't resist asking the question. "How do you know each other?"

"We are family friends. Our parents are business partners"

"Just friends?" he blabbered.

Siddanth witted "yes!,,, just friends!,,,,,,, I heard you are treating Prisha today. Can I join the party?" Siddanth smiled.

Pranav thought in mind Idiot! You are asking treat for free and sitting with my girl but he smiled and said "ya sure. I am truly grateful. Prisha definitely needs this treat. She has helped me to pass my exam"

Prisha ordered snacks and cool drinks. "Cheers" they had their drink.

"So where are you from? I mean place?" asked Siddanth.

"I am from Mumbai. What about you?" replied Pranav.

"We are from Bangalore" Siddanth grinned looking at Prisha. "Why did you choose medicine?"

"Actually I was forced to join. I had no intention of becoming a doctor" Pranav gazed at the coffee in reticence.

"Then what you wanted to do?"

"I have no idea. Frankly speaking, I don't have any aim in my life. After plus 2 exams, my father questioned me. I looked at him blankly. I was clueless. My father suggested me to follow his footsteps and become a doctor. I was brought here to this prestigious institution. I got admission, but I still feel hollow. The new faces, big textbooks, difficult terminologies mocked at me.

I wondered why I came here. To see dead bodies and cutting them to see what is inside? I feel nauseating holding test tubes with urine samples.

I couldn't believe I was holding urine of some other person, trying to estimate what it contains.

Was it for this purpose I came to this world? I still feel I am missing something and I still don't know what it is! My twenty years of life was like an orchestrated choreography.

Why was I created? The enigmatic question often provokes my mind. I may sound too philosophical, but at one point of time, everybody feels the same. Everybody run in a marathon of life pursuing their goals and when they finally achieve it, what next? Another marathon till we become old and die?

Happiness is what you seek and this happiness is different for each one of us." He just sat quiet staring across the window.

"You sound philosophical. I can just say, you came to this world to serve the needy." Siddanth tried to convince him.

Serve the needy, my foot. But he grinned and said "Yes may be. I have some work, I need to go" Pranav walked out without saying a bye.

Siddanth and Prisha looked at each other unbelievingly.

Three days had passed and Pranav was missing. He was absent for all the classes.

"What happened to him? Is he sick?" Prisha enquired his roommate.

"Pranav has gone home" he replied.

"But why?"

"I have no idea! He just packed his bags and left"

"Something is wrong with this guy" she felt pity.

After one week Pranav was back to college. He sat solemn in class and spent the evening in solitude.

Prisha met him in a corridor. "I need to talk to you. Can we?" she looked in his eyes.

"Yes" he nodded.

"Where have you been, you just disappeared! Your room mate said,, you had gone home. What happened? Any problem?" she thundered with questions. "I thought you were sick. Actually I was worried"

He looked at her and there was some bliss in his face. "I had been to Baba ashram."

"Baba ashram?"

"He is revered as fountain of love, strength and wisdom. I find peace and I get illuminated in his presence"

Prisha couldn't understand the altered sense of him. A medical student was aspiring to become a disciple of some Baba? She couldn't comprehend anything.

"Then why did you come back. You should have stayed in that ashram and should have been one among his disciples!" she snorted.

"Yes I would like that. I think I was born to serve the needy. I have to become a doctor and serve the poor" he said blankly.

"Good! Nice thought. Shall we walk to the class then?"

"Of course"

First year of medicine was over. Pranav had passed with good grades. It was because of Prisha. She had taught him to a great extent. Their friendship was blooming. During that period, Prisha noticed some mood swings in his behavior. Either he would be too polite and peaceful or showered his arrogance and tantrums.

He had started loving her for her patience. But, he couldn't t tolerate her friendship with Siddanth. Jealousy crept inside him like a poisonous snake.

It was 'ETHNIC DAY' celebration in college. The Girls and boys had an opportunity to celebrate the diversity of vibrant and colorful India. They wore traditional attire. Girls looked gorgeous with their colorful sarees, each depicting their own state. The boys matched in par with kurtas and dhotis. The open air auditorium was decorated with flowers and lamps. Rangolis and pookalams welcomed the audiences.

A fashion show was organized and a best dressed male and female were to be awarded. Siddanth and Pranav waited patiently. At last Prisha came in a beautiful red chiffon saree. She was mesmerizing.

WHAT A BEAUTY!!!!!!!!! Pranav felt like kissing her and adoring her.

"So guys,, how do I look?" she asked cheerfully.

'hmnnn ok… nothing great!" Siddanth tantalized.

"Really? Show me a beauty queen then? She retorted.

Pranav wanted to express his feelings,, YOU LOOK GORGEOUS,, LIKE AN ANGEL but his lips were locked and he stood in a trance.

Prisha walked off towards the girl's team. The fashion show started and girls walked on the ramp flaunting their sarees. The boys were no less and stood in brilliance.

The function was culminating and it was time to give away the awards.

"THE BEST DRESSED FEMALE,, IS,,, a great silence.

The candidates kept their fingers crossed, and then it was called,, PRISHA……..

Prisha was terribly surprised and she hurried with scurrying feet towards the stage. She took the trophy and kissed it and then she walked on the ramp again.

"Now…. It's time for BEST DRESSED MALE,,,, the crowd was cheering again. And its,,,, SIDDANTH,,,!"

Siddanth ran over the stage and took the trophy. Prisha hugged him and said CONGRATULATIONS!!!!.. "same to you" he cheered her. Both stood flaunting their trophies.

The crowd had only one thought,,, WOW,, A BEST COUPLE,,,,

Pranav was livid and the jealousy crept inside him like a snake burning his every emotion. His mind was in turmoil and the envy burned like a forest fire.

Two years passed. It was graduation day.

'Last day ever' the students thought and they were proud of each other. They remembered the time of togetherness.

Funny anecdotes about stupid things and flashes of stories blast through their mind. They reminisced their five years. They all looked back to see how they felt during dissection of cadavers, testing urine samples, seeing pink and blue slides, taking patient histories. It was never ending. Some cherished and others wanted to get out of monotonous workout.

Prisha sat on a bench and tears rolled down her cheeks.

"Why are you crying buddy? Cheer up. You must be proud that I am graduating today" Siddanth grinned.

"This is your last day in campus" she cried.

"Yes last day, but I am stepping out for a new beginning. You must be happy"

"I will miss you" she hugged him.

"I will miss you too. This is not an end. We will meet again. I promise" he tried pacifying.

"You are moving out to another country pursuing higher studies. I hope you will remember me"

"You are my special friend, Prisha,,,, and I can never forget you. I will come back" he gave her a warm hug.

An announcement was made and Students had to assemble near the podium. The dean gave his final speech.

Siddanth walked towards the podium with head held high and chest puffed up. He received "best outgoing student" award, and what else he could ask for.

The day ended with blur and tears.

Siddanth left and Prisha felt hollow from inside. She faced a gloomy hue and she missed him from her bottom of her heart.

Destiny had other plans and she hoped she would get another chance to relive all the happy memories that his friendship had given her.

Chapter 3

THE AUDITORIUM WAS HUGE AND glittered with ceremony. Prominent personalities had arrived from various states of India. The hall was buzzing with activity. The stage was set to honor eminent journalists in various categories.

The function began with traditional lightning of lamp and Invocations were sung to lord Ganesha, the god who eliminates all difficulties and help humans to progress.

Various speakers spoke about the media and the impact it had on the people. There were many nominations and also a life time achievement award was about to be given.

The program began with a great applause.

The nominated journalists kept their fingers crossed. I AM GOING TO WIN,, each one thought.

After the life time achievement award,, it was time for other categories,,, and the award for the year 2015 Best Feature Journalist goes to……. A silence,,,,,,,,, Nynisha.

There was a great applause and the crowd cheered. Nynisha ran towards the stage to receive the award when,,,,,

The alarm rang. She woke up from that incomplete dream

She looked at the clock and snorted "couldn't you wait till I finished my dream?"

The door knocked and her mother called her. She looked at the clock and reckoned about her appointments of the day and hurried towards the bathroom.

Nynisha was a journalist and she had struggled to become one. Parvathi, Nynisha s mother was a friendly woman. She had taken great care in pursuing her children s career. She was a great cook too.

Nynisha was a charming lady and her smile encouraged other smiles. Her pleasant countenance exuded her. She spread joy around her and beautified her world. She had a long silky hair which almost touched her bottom. Her Friends had nick named her as "Rapunzel". She had won many prizes contesting for the most wonderful and beautiful hair in college.

Boys of her age adored her and had made an attempt to propose her.

"Nynisha, I love your beautiful hair. Will you marry me?"

"Nynisha, I love you more than my soul. I can't live without you!"

"Before I met you, I never realized how empty my life was!"

"I wish I could give you everything, but I hope this ring will be enough!"

Such proposals had become common to her. She tactfully handled each of them with her bewitched beauty. On one occasion, her senior batch mate had proposed her with flowers and chocolates. She couldn't resist those dark chocolates. She quietly took them and ate. Later she said "sorry buddy, only chocolates were good" and had walked off.

She was a great writer and she wrote with brilliance. She often wrote to the college magazines. She wanted to bring revolution through her writing. She made the youngsters to reckon. She had a great impulse to learn, listen to stories of the people and promulgate them.

She did her post-graduation from a leading school of journalism. She had joined as a journalist in an established magazine. Her articles were commendable.

Nynisha peered into the mirror and was busy brushing her teeth. She heard the knock on the door. "Gosh! It s mom! I need to clean up the mess before mom peeps inside" she hurried with a broom and cleaned the papers. She tried making it tidy in short time.

"Nynisha, it's time for the yoga class. Come soon. I am waiting" said her mother sharply.

Nynisha was ready within minutes and came to the living room. "Good morning mom!"

"Good morning dear! It's late, let's hurry!" Parvathi fondly hugged her. They started their morning stroll. It was dawn and the sun rays brightened the roads. She remembered her dream. She wished it would come true.

"Mom, I had a wonderful dream. I was receiving an award for best featured journalist when suddenly, the stupid alarm broke in" Nynisha said lividly.

"You should not start your day with anger my child. Take deep breaths, relax for a moment. I have heard morning dreams come true,, lets pray" Parvathi grinned

Nynisha took deep breaths. The early morning oxygen felt good to her lungs. "I feel better"

"Good. What did you think of that proposal which I told yesterday?"

"Proposal?"

"Yes, marriage proposal"

"I wonder why mothers always think of their daughter marriage. I can't marry now. I am just building up my career. I need some more time,,,,, please" Nynisha persuaded.

"Career and family life should go hand in hand. Gone are the days when women were mere housewives and looked after the house hold chores. Women have grown in every field creating a par excellence with men. I appreciate your contribution to this society. But I am also a mother and I have the right to dream about your future."

They reached the yoga center. It was a small hall but artistically decorated for the purpose of meditation. A caption on the wall read

"yoga for life. Free your mind, body and soul"

Nynisha placed her mat. She started warming up by stretching. She started with initial lotus pose and performed pranayam, asana, kriya and chanted mantra. Her senses enlightened. She felt rejuvenated.

They were back to their home and Nynisha had to hurry. She didn't want to hear loathing remarks of her boss. She had several papers to be finished. As a journalist by profession, she was running around day in and day out.

"Mom, I am getting late. I will have breakfast in the office" said Nynisha frantically. She hurried towards the door.

Parvathi made a toast in a hurry and burnt her fingers. She bellowed.

Nynisha dropped her things and ran towards her mother. She immersed Parvathi s hand in ice water and applied antiseptic ointment. "Be careful mom"

She kissed her mother and walked out. She approached her car and was abashed. It was looking worse with all the mud on it. She hurriedly cleaned her car and sat inside. She tried to start the engine, but in vain. The car stubbornly stood unshaken.

"I forgot to get the car serviced. I have to service my brain too" she jabbed her head in frustration.

She hurried for a taxi.

"Driver hurry, I am already late" Nynisha said in trepidation.

The traffic was horrible and the driver struggled to find his way. After some time, the road cleared and he pressed on the accelerator. The car zoomed in.

A black sedan followed her and came close hitting the taxi.

The driver noticed in rear view mirror and made a sudden turn. The wheels skidded hitting a tree. Nynisha pounced to the front seat. The bumper was jammed.

She was shocked for a moment. She tried focusing on the number plate of black sedan, but it quickly pulled off. She looked at the driver. He was baffled too.

"Are you okay?" she asked him

"I think so,,, my car!,,,, What will I tell my boss?" he was frantic.

"Did you see the number plate?"

"No,,, It happened so fast,,, it was some black sedan" the driver said blankly.

"We will lodge a FIR. Come quick". She took him to a police station and lodged a complaint. She looked at the watch "I will surely get fired!" she thought.

She hurried for another taxi.

The office was situated in a sub urban locality. It was a nice ten story building. The magazine "Verity" was known to promulgate everything that matters. It covered news, business, arts, life, cookery, people, sport, cartoons. It had grown indistinctly. People loved the magazine. Hotly debated issues, valid concerns, ridiculous opinion were all published. It presented events from diverse point of view, liberal, democrat. In short, it was a world at a glance.

George Patrick was the owner of the magazine. Running the business and managing several projects had created a weak havoc in his mindset. He had become unpredictable with his mood swings. The employees had to tolerate the savvy boss. But nevertheless, he always showed his attitude constantly.

He was short and stout, yet truly stubborn. He constantly read newspapers, magazines and often searched the web. In a world with different sources of media like television, web, newspapers, "verity" magazine had to survive. It was a paramount. He respected the readers and made the articles clear.

Sometimes he growled and passed loathing comments on his workers. He howled incessantly and sinisterly and got the work done in time. Time was a precious factor indeed and he hated late comers and journalists who didn't finish their work in time.

He pressed the button on his desk. His secretary came bashing through the door. "Call Nynisha, Tell her, to get the report quickly" snapped George.

"Sure sir!" mumbled the secretary Jisha.

Jisha hurried towards Nynisha s cabin. It was empty. Nynisha had not yet arrived. "Oh she is not here! God save her soul!" she thought.

"What to tell boss?" Jisha pondered. She hesitantly walked towards George s cabin and gingerly opened the door.

He cocked his brow "what?" he said.

"Nynisha has not yet arrived" she spoke lowly.

George was agitated. He looked at his watch and he grew crimson. "When the moron arrives, tell her to see me immediately" he snapped.

Nynisha arrived late and sat in her cabin. She was panting. She opened a bottle to drink water when Jisha broke in "When the moron arrives, tell her to see me immediately" Jisha mimicked her boss.

"He called me a moron! How dare he? I am late, but I have a reason" snarled Nynisha.

"I hope you don't get fired" Jisha grinned

Nynisha glowered but her conscience told her to calm down. She breathed a heavy sigh and slowly walked to his cabin.

She knocked the door resentfully. "May I come in" she asked sharply.

"Yes" replied George.

Her presence increased his vexation. "What time are you supposed to come to office? You know that, I hate late comers"

"I am sorry Sir! Actually I met with an accident in the morning"

"Accident? But, you look fine" he tantalized.

"Idiot! You wanted me to call from hospital with all broken bones?" she thought.

"Some black sedan came hitting close to my taxi and my driver jammed to a tree. Luckily, I am fine" she said indignantly.

"Did you file a FIR?"

"Yes"

"ok,,,, where are the papers? Did you complete assignment?"

"How in human!"

She placed the papers on his table. He looked at it and said "get back to work"

Nynisha walked out in frustration "He is disgusting! I wonder why I am still stuck up with this magazine." She sat in her cabin reckoning about the events and interviews she need to confront. The work load was getting hectic day by day.

Athira entered her cabin. "You look awful! What happened?"

"A bad day, my mom burnt her fingers in the morning. I stayed back, giving her first aid. Then my car didn't start. I took a cab and I met with an accident"

"You met with an accident! Where? when? how?" Athira gabbled.

"Relax. A black sedan came hitting close to my cab and the driver hit a tree. The bumper was jammed and the stupid old boss calls me a moron for coming late! How could he? I reckon we are working here because we have a good IQ!" Nynisha said defiantly.

"Oh! What a plight! Nynisha, I cannot imagine more,,,,,," Athira was pacifying.

Jisha entered the cabin "Boss is calling Athira".

"I think, it's my turn" she said warily and went to his cabin.

Nynisha sat gloomily peering into the computer screen.

It was lunch time. Nynisha s stomach made hunger sounds. She had missed her breakfast. She went to the canteen. There were loads of dishes on the menu. She ordered and waited impatiently.

She gobbled like a hungry cat, until she had a burp.

Athira joined "You couldn't wait for me? I had bought nice cookies for you"

"Sorry dear. I was very hungry. I had missed my breakfast. I couldn't resist the food. I just gobbled whatever possible!" Nynisha said airily and looked at the cookies in Athira s hand. "Give me the cookies"

"You just ate like a pig and you have place for this cookie too?" Athira was flabbergasted.

"Yep! I can have them!" Nynisha immediately gulped them. "It's delicious! You are like my mom."

"Thanks. So have you started cooking?" asked Athira. "Cooking and me? Impossible! I just love to eat and not to cook." Nynisha said merrily.

"I pity your future husband and children. Any ways, look,,,,, I have got something to show you" Athira took out a small paper from her bag. Nynisha opened the folded paper.

Inside were a few words which looked like a scribbling of a young child.

Dear Sunitha miss.

You look hot and sexy in that pink saree. All my friends Adi, Rijwal, Prasanth love you. But I love you the most. you are very pretty. When I become big, I will marry you.

Nynisha guffawed at the letter. "I reckon this is your tiny tot Rohan s first love letter!" she chuckled.

"Can you imagine how a ten year old boy can get such thoughts? I was startled! I got this letter in his homework book. He had kept it hiding. I don't know how to handle him!" Athira was disturbed.

"You need to be calm and gentle. Look into his sensitivity. Teach him the right way. You have to cut down on television. The programs have great impact on them. This love letter is one of the outcomes. Peer pressure also adds up to his behavior. You can discuss with his class teacher"

Jisha broke in "boss is calling"

Nynisha cocked her brow "not again!"

She gave a warm hug to Athira "will catch up evening. I have to get ready to meet the devil!" she grinned.

Chapter 4

Tom sat on a small rock and faced the horizon. The early morning sky was mesmerizing. The sun was about to rise. The sky slowly changed its colors from black to orange to blue. The orange ball slowly peeped above.

A new day was beginning, bringing misfortune to some.

Only vengeance prevailed in his heart. Life had become merciless. Pain and sorrow went hand in hand with him. The cruel, relentless people ruled this world.

His head was still aching, but he had lot of things to complete.

He slowly opened his diary and wrote,,,

> To sin is to invite misery
> And for that invitation
> I am glad to redeem
> What you deserve
> For the pain you have caused me
> I pledge to destroy you all
> One by one.......
> ,,,,,,,,, one by one

He closed his eyes and he saw a flash back,,,

He was running deep inside a forest. He searched in vain and desperation crept through him. But he had reached too late.

Too late to undo anything that had happened.

It was then, the retribution was born.

He slowly remembered the events of the previous day.

He searched for a few names in a social network. He could retrieve only a few.

He phoned his friends and acquired some information. He began his game plan. He wrote a network of people on a wall interconnecting them with lines and the way to execute them all.

Tom heard a voice kill those bastards

Tom sat in a corner of a pub, serenely brooding on his own private thought. The bartender served him a cocktail. At the other end he noticed two strangers, busy in their talk. A third one joined.

Tom looked at the third person in surprise and his eyes burned in anger. His vengeance increased the pace of his heart. He expected every moment to see his dead face.

He was Sijas,,,,, his first target.

The men had a brief talk and exchanged briefcases. Sijas quickly walked out.

Sijas looked contended as he placed the briefcase in his bike. He drove towards the exit of the city. He reached a hilly terrain and slowed his bike on the curvy roads.

Tom silently followed him.

Sijas ascended up on a steep muddy road. The tiny rocks interrupted the tires and it was a challenging path to ascend up. The undulating road was never ending and was leading to a cliff.

The rugged sharp rocks beneath the cliff were a welcome sign of death. The sea waves splashed on the rocks mystifying the nature

It was night and hardly anything was visible. Sijas rode with difficulty. After a humpy bumpy ride, he reached an old dilapidated house at the top of the cliff. The house was well covered by trees and plantations.

Sijas knocked the door of that old house and someone welcomed him.

Tom silently followed him. He hid himself near a tree and used his binoculars to focus on the house. He moved his hand and caught sight of a window. The room was faintly lit and he noticed vague figures moving around.

Three men looked happy, as Sijas opened a briefcase before them. They cheered and hugged each other. They opened up beer cans to have fun. One of the men offered Sijas a small package. He opened and poured its contents on his hand. The sparkling diamonds glittered in the faint light.

The second man opened a small box and Sijas found packets of cocaine. He sniffed some to feel the ecstasy.

Tom looked on in awe as the gang had fun.

Sijas received a phone call and he walked out of house with a torch. He trotted down a narrow path and stood at the edge of the cliff. He carefully looked into his binoculars towards the sea. He noticed something and he waved the torch giving a signal. He then hurried downhill in a jeep.

Tom ran towards the edge of cliff and looked into binoculars. A small ship was heading towards the shore. 'A new assignment must be coming' Tom thought.

Tom hurried downhill.

The small ship halted in the sea, a few miles away from the shore. Sijas parked his jeep near a rock and hurried towards a motorboat. He started the engine and zoomed into the sea towards the ship. He arrived close to ship.

A few men on top of the ship tied two boxes with a rope and slowly dropped them down into the motorboat. Sijas carefully placed those boxes and drove back towards the shore.

He reached the shore and tied the motor boat to a rock and loaded the boxes into the jeep. He quickly drove uphill.

Tom looked on in surprise and pondered over his next move. He drove his bike with cheerful and beaming eyes as he had found his first target.

He decided to keep a watch on Sijas for few days and devise a plan.

Everyday Sijas drove downhill and visited different pubs in city. He collected goods from the sea and distributed them. It was his routine.

Tom fidgeted with his pen and then he drew a sketch in his diary. He looked at the picture and smiled viciously.

The next day he filled two cans with oil. He drove towards the hilly terrain. He parked his bike behind a tree and carried the two cans.

'It was night and Sijas would be arriving downhill' he thought. Tom noticed a light moving downhill. He quickly spilled the two cans of oil on the road. He hid himself behind a tree.

Tom waited to see his death.

Sijas drove downhill. He was happy. He had got a wonderful assignment. Lots of money he thought. He merrily sang a song.

He drove his bike and felt a merry time was arriving. Suddenly, the wheels skidded and he lost his balance. He tried controlling, but the road was slimy.

He was at the edge of the cliff.

The bike fell and was caught in a tree. Sijas struggled in a thorn bush. The thorns pricked him making him cry for help. He looked up and saw someone standing.

He cried,, "help me,, please,, help"

Tom laughed sinisterly.

"You deserve death and nothing else,,, met your maker with a split skull" Tom said.

Sijas couldn't make out Tom in the dark. He wondered who it could be. He screeched for help. The thorny bush gave way and he fell down on the rocks.

Thud,,,

The sound was heard and Tom laughed hysterically.

My first target dead!

Good job Tom, now next! His master said

Tom heard a voice commanding him. He felt the voice was of his godfather.

Tom quickly escaped from the place.

It was 11 pm night. He saw a local bar. He was happy and he wanted to celebrate alone. He entered the bar, ordered a peg of whisky and sat on a table. He curled his lips as he sipped the alcohol.

He remembered how he had executed Sijas.

Tom was completely intoxicated. He dawdled on the road with a whisky bottle in his hand. He was disoriented and he walked into the highway. A car collided on him and escaped. The last thing he remembered was of shattering noise of his broken whiskey bottle.

Tom fell on the ground with an injured head.

A few people near the bar noticed the accident and quickly took him to a nearby hospital.

Now he sat alone, remembering the hospital incident. His left hand hit him again. He heard a voice "damn you! How can you be so careless? You have lot of work to do. Targets to be fixed. You cannot die in a road accident without completing the tasks. The hell is waiting for the bastards and you should lead them the way"

"Yes, I need to be careful" he thought.

His head was aching and his left hand slapped him. Tom was getting annoyed with his left hand. It had continued doing absurd things. It was really getting out of his control.

Tom remembered the saying

"Miles to go before I sleep."

He climbed down the rocks and was ready for the next task.

He reached home.

His anxiety didn't allow him to sleep. He rolled on the bed. Late in the mid night he suddenly woke up with a scream and his face was perspiring. He had seen the same vicious dream of childhood.

He was young and innocent and weak. He couldn't resist the harm he underwent during that small age. His fear had grown with time. Now he had become a young man with retribution and vengeance in his mind.

HOW CAN YOU FORGET ABOUT HIM. FIND HIM WHERE IS HE. HE IS SUPPOSED TO BE KILLED. GET UP, YOU MORON. YOU GOT LOT TO DO.

Tom opened the cupboard and peered into the old files. With each file, memories came flashing across. With trembling hands he took out a photo. Tears rolled down his cheeks.

'I miss you" he said and cried at the photo
He lamented until his emotions subsided.

Tom looked at his old toy cars and dolls. Every child cherishes his or her own childhood memories, but for him, childhood had become a horror movie.

As he searched he got a photo. His eyes turned red and he set the photo ablaze

For the sin you did, death is the only answer. I am coming.

Chapter 5

After seven long years, Siddanth saw Prisha in a supermarket. They stared at each other in disbelief. Time had changed many things.

He gave her a warm embrace. "I tried contacting you. Your father said you moved out to another state for post graduation. He even said you got married. I didn't want to disturb the newly married couple. Later,,, I got busy with my career. Time just flew"

Her eyes welled up in tears.

"Please don't cry. I have kept my promise. I am back. So who is the lucky guy?" he grinned.

She replied with heaviness in her heart "I got married to Pranav"

"What? You married that idiot? I can't believe. I know you were batch mates, but never expected you would fall for him" he staggered.

"It just happened. I can't explain how and why" she said lowly.' so,,, where are you staying and where are you working?"

"I am working in 'We Care' hospital as a psychiatrist and what about you?"

"So you are psyched up!" Prisha guffawed. "I am working as senior resident in department of medicine in Silon hospital.

"That's great! We are in same town now. Should we do all the talking in this market or can we go somewhere?"

Prisha was about to say yes, when her phone rang. Her expression changed. She quickly pulled out a card and scribbled something on it.

"Sorry Siddanth, I have to go. This is my card. Will call you soon"

Siddanth could sense it.

Something was wrong.

Siddanth tried calling her but she never picked up the phone and never answered his messages.

His instincts told him something was really wrong. He went to Silon hospital. He enquired in the reception. Prisha had not turned up to the hospital since two days. He quickly glanced at the card, which she had given. She had written her house address at the back. He hurried towards her house.

He rang the bell, but no one answered. He even knocked the door. No response. He was about to leave when he heard shattering of a glass from inside. He ran towards the window to check.

As he peeped through the window, he stood shocked. Prisha was lying on the floor. He shouted Prisha!

Prisha was too weak to even get up. She just looked at him.

Siddanth tried from the back door. The latch was loose and the door opened. Siddanth ran inside towards her. The sight was aghast. Prisha had bruises all over. Her eyes were swollen.

Siddanth quickly picked her up in his arms and hurried towards hospital. She was admitted in intensive care, until she recovered.

Siddanth took great care of her.

Prisha sat on the bed sipping coffee.

"Thank god! You now look good. My beautiful Prisha is back." He gave a friendly hug.

She smiled and said "thank you"

"Prisha, I just want to know everything, every single detail. What the hell is happening in your life?" Siddanth frowned.

She closed her eyes and the horrifying incidents swayed across. Then she spoke

"My life changed as you moved out of the campus. I felt miserable and hollow.

I was emotionally down and that was the time Pranav took great care of me. We become good friends. We studied together, went to restaurants together. I don't know when I fell for him. We were in love. Everything was beautiful. Happiness was back.

We completed the final year. Pranav s grades were bad in all the semesters. I was getting distinction in all the years. Inferiority complex crept inside him. Things started to change. He couldn't accept his failure. His behavior was changing.

But I always stood by him.

He was domineering and sarcastic at times. He became over possessive about me. He never tolerated if I spoke to other men.

It was suffocating, but, I loved him

Our college life ended. We were out of the campus. But we met often in libraries. He never studied though. By god's grace I secured a good rank and took post-graduation in medicine.

He felt dejected and broken. He couldn't perform well in exam. He went into solitude for few days. I had to leave him and pursued my career.

My father had one more cardiac arrest. Luckily he survived. But anxiety had crept in him. My father wanted to witness my marriage before he died. He brought in many good marriage proposals.

My love for Pranav had masked my emotions and sentiments. I just rejected every proposal.

One day, my father called me. He was bedridden with diarrhea. "Prisha, I don't know when will be my last breath. It may be today or tomorrow."

I couldn't hear those words "Dad, please don't say that" and I cried bitterly.

"Prisha, you have rejected all those proposals. If you love someone, please tell. I will be happy to know about that"

I decided to tell the truth and I slowly muttered. "I love Pranav. He is my batch mate."

"Why didn't you tell me that before?"

"I couldn't dad"

"Call him tomorrow. I have to speak to him"

The meeting went on well and Pranav made sure that dad would like him by his magical words.

My father was happy to have him as a son in law.

Both the families met and discussed about marriage ceremonies. We finally got married. We had been to Shimla for our honeymoon. It was the most fascinating moments, I must say. The revelry lasted only for a few days.

The last day of my honeymoon, I got a call from my house. My dad had passed away. The loss of my father was intensely unbearable.

I crumbled.

We came back to offer our last rights to him.

It was the beginning of doom in my life. A bad omen had started.

Two weeks after my father s death, I decided to return to college to complete my post graduation. I still remember the taunting remarks of my husband.

"You are so insensitive. You lost your dad just two weeks back and now you are moving ahead without a least concern on me. All those cries and gloomy feelings were hypocrisy. You were mocking it to the world."

His sinister remarks vexed me. "Shut up! Don't you dare speak anymore. I am not a hypocrite and I need not explain to you or to the world, what love I had to my father."

But his sneering remarks continued. "I don't want you to go. Stay here till I get through exam"

His words bruised my ego. "God knows, when you will succeed. I don't think morons can pass through!" I walked out after that duel.

After two days my vexation had reduced and I called him.

"Why are you calling?" He snarled.

"I am sorry Pranav, but think rationally. I cannot waste time. Please understand. I am sure you will acquire it by next year. You need to have some patience. Put your hard work and I am sure, you will succeed."

Pranav just banged the phone. The call ended.

I called him several times, but his phone was switched off. I decided not to pester him anymore.

Pranav used to visit me whenever his hormones surged. His sexual appetite was never ending. We decided to buy a rental house and we started living together.

My marriage had lost the complete meaning of a good relationship. I was not able to tolerate his lackadaisical attitude. I wanted to understand the crux of his problem and solve it, but he never allowed that.

He passed his time watching porn movies and what not. At night he wanted to experiment on me. Another year passed. Life was becoming really difficult. He didn't even attend the entrance exam.

If I asked about it, he would just say "mind your own business".

His behavior had changed distinctly. He would threaten neighborhood men. He often checked my phone messages. The phone log account was checked. He wanted every detail. Who called me, whom I called, everything!

As I returned from hospital, he would snatch my bag and do the searching. If he found a coffee bill, he would howl "with whom did you have coffee?"

Any new dress in my cupboard would trigger him. "Who gifted you?"

If he saw a car outside our house, he would walk around with great suspicion. "Somebody is waiting for you. Don't go!" he would scream.

He had become insane.

He required psychiatric consultation. He never obliged to visit any.

One day, he saw me with Dr Arun. He was my colleague. We were off rounds. The suspicion grew inside him. The same day he followed me. He saw us in hypermarket. Your warm embrace vexed him.

Do you remember, I received a call when I met you? It was Pranav. He threatened to commit suicide. So I had to hurry.

When I reached home, Pranav was berserk and gave an impetuous look at me."You are a bitch. I knew it. I saw you with Dr Arun in the morning and now you are meeting your old boy friend Dr Siddanth. I know he has come back to take you away.

You are just like my mother. A whore! You seduce the men around you with your beauty. My father divorced my mom, because she was a whore. I hated all women. I hate you too. You are all same......... whores"

I couldn't bear his savaging remarks and I slapped him.

He became hysterical and battered me. I was about to die. You saved me.

Prisha wiped her tears. Siddanth stood speechless and hugged her. He didn't know what to say. "We grew up dreaming wonderful things. But life plays its own game. You should be strong in difficult times. I really appreciate your perseverance for holding on to such a mad man. He is insane. I surmise that he had a bad childhood experience. He never got his motherly love and his dad fed him with all wrong things in his brain. So he started hating women. He suffered from morbid jealousy or you can say a deadly passion against you. Actually, you have become Desdemona of Othello."

Chapter 6

————— ◆◆◆ —————

IT WAS A SUNDAY. ATHIRA, Rahul and Rohan were having fun in the house. Athira had cooked scrumptious delicacies. "Lunch is ready,,,," she yelled fondly at her husband and her son.

They were about to have lunch when the main door was knocked.

"Hello! Athira I have brought delicious custard for Rohan. I know he loves it!" an old lady said amicably.

"Oh! Thanks aunt Indira. Please do join us for lunch" Athira said airily.

"oh!oh! It's ok I finished with that old man" she made a mocking face.

Indira left the house.

"We are lucky to have a friendly neighbor. Rohan was missing his grandparents. May be, god sent these old couple" Athira grinned and looked at her husband.

Athira had got new neighbors. She took time to understand them. But, something always mystified her. She heard temple bells, chains rattling and some hymns. She wondered what the old couple often did in their house.

When she questioned, the old couple had replied that they were performing some rituals. It was their old tradition.

Weeks passed.

One day Athira was fidgeting "Rohan s birthday is arriving. Lot of work is pending. I need your help" she eyed at her husband.

"Don't worry Athira. I have already booked the party hall and decided about party lunch" Rahul said flatly.

"How can you decide on the lunch alone? You didn't even bother to ask me?" Athira retorted.

"Relax Athira; I know your taste and your likings. I have booked accordingly." He pacified her.

They spent the rest of the day inviting their friends, for the birthday party. Rohan was excited as he would be getting many gifts.

They visited the old couple. As they entered the house, an aromatic perfume engulfed their nostrils. The house was freaky with odd stuff. A huge idol of goddess kali was kept in the center. The goddess was surrounded by some old photos. Camphor was burnt and they were doing a special pooja.

Athira and Rahul felt weird at the sight.

"These are our ancestors. We worship them daily. We pray for their well being in heaven" the old couple said precisely.

Odd traditional customs

Athira and her husband exchanged looks and spoke nonchalantly "that's fine. We came to invite you for our Rohan s birthday party. Please do come." Athira grinned.

"Oh sure, Rohan is like our grandson. How can we miss it? We will be there on time" Indira said silkily

Rohan had a blast on his birthday party. The cake was fabulous with two layers one of chocolate and another of vanilla, moist and tasty. The frosting was of real butter cream. All the arrangement made by the organizers was excellent. They had arranged a magic show, games for toddlers and young children. A musical chair was played cheerfully by the children. A mini dance show was performed by school students who were Rohan s cousins.

The party was a great fun. Rohan received fantastic toys and video games as gifts. He was mesmerized and jubilant.

One day, Athira was returning from her work. She saw Indira walking with groceries in her hand. She thought of soliciting help and approached her.

She was about to say "hello" when suddenly Indira felt dizzy and fell on the road.

Athira was baffled for a second. She swiftly neared her and took her in her arms.

"Aunt Indira,,,, what happened?" she asked in anxiety.

Indira spoke in a confused manner. Her words were incorrigible.

"I am not able to understand,,, what are you saying?" Athira turned around and saw Rohan playing in the far corner of the street.

She yelled at her son and he quickly came running. "Call your dad fast,,, Indira aunty not well,, we need to take her home

Rohan ran and brought his dad along with him. Athira and Rahul took Indira to her house. The old man looked on worried.

"Indira aunty is feeling dizzy and she is speaking in a confused tone. I will call a doctor soon" Athira took her phone to dial a number.

The old man stopped her "no,,, thanks for your help,, I will take care of her. She must be too tired. Old age problems,,, you see"

"But,, she needs to be checked" Athira spoke in apprehension.

"I will call my family doctor,,, please" the old man called someone on the phone.

"We will wait till you get help" Athira pacified the old man

"I can take care of my wife,,, you please leave" the old man said gruffly

"How can you be so rude,,, we were trying to help you out" Athira retorted

Rahul stopped Athira "it's their family matter,,, let's leave"

Athira and family walked out vexed.

The following day Athira was busy making breakfast when she heard a knock on the door. She opened and was surprised to see Indira.

"I apologize,,, I know my husband was rude at you,,, he is a cranky old man,,, he doesn't know how to behave with people,, old age has increased his frustration"

"That's fine,, aunty,,, so,, how are you? What happened to you yesterday?"

"Sometimes my vision gets blurred,, I will talk in a nonsense manner,, I feel dazed and get severe headache,,, I am going for a checkup today,,, let's see,, what the doc will say" Indira frowned

"Oh,,, shall I accompany you?" Athira was ready to help.

"I know you have a savvy boss,,, and you can't take off,,
I will take care,,, once again,,, thanks for your help" Indira
held Athira s hand in gratitude

"You are like my mother,,, I am ready to help you,, any
day" Athira grinned

Indira smiled and took a taxi. She went to hospital.

Chapter 7

THE SUN RAYS PRICKED HER eyes. Nynisha awoke lazily and yawned. "Thank god! It's a holiday!" she thought. She dawdled towards the kitchen for a coffee when suddenly she heard her brother yelling in adjacent room. She peeped in to check.

Nishan was shouting over the phone "get it aborted!" His voice was gruff and his brows were drawn together in a frown.

Nynisha was baffled, she quickly confronted him.

"What the hell!,, what did you just speak?" she howled.

"Nynisha,, ny-ni-sha,," he stammered and turned silent.

"I am asking who is on the phone! Answer me right now!" She snapped.

"It's Pratheeksha,,, my girlfriend,, we did a mistake,,,,, she,,,, she is pregnant! I don't know what to do? We have exams coming up next month,, and this shit of pregnancy,,,, I am getting nervous,,,," Nishan stammered. His face was gaunt and sunken.

"Are you out of your mind? You have done a mistake,, and you call this pregnancy a shit!,,,,,, it's your baby…. I feel like chastising you,,,,, is this for mom and dad sent you to college,,,, to go on fucking and making babies,,, you were sent to become an architect! Mind you,,,,," Nynisha was red with anger.

"Nynisha,,, please,,,, I don't have a choice,, Prateeksha can't have this baby!,,,, she can't run around in the campus with a full blown stomach,,,, our friends will mock at us,, and this society,,,," Nishan was fidgeting. His eyes were red in tears.

"You are worried about what your friends will say?,, what the society will think of you?,,,, you never realized what pain it will cost our parents,,,, what have you done is brazen!" Nynisha affronted him.

"What is done is done! I cannot undo it,,,,, I need a solution now,,,, and the only solution is abortion,,," he said gravelly.

Nynisha slapped him hard "Just shut up! I wonder why you don't have the slightest remorse for the act you have done!" she looked into his eyes fiercely.

Nishan stood frozen.

"Don't you dare talk any more,, I will try sorting it out" She slumped on the chair in agony.

After an hour of reckoning she spoke sternly. "Look, if she is pregnant now,,,, it will take nine more months to deliver. Right now, you please concentrate on your studies and complete your exams. I surmise that your exams will be over by another six weeks. Anyhow, this is your last semester. You won't visit your college again except to collect your degree certificates and graduation. I will speak to mom and dad about this. You both are going to get married in another two or three months. So,,,, when legally you both are husband and wife,,, you won't have problem with this child,,"

"Marriage! How can I,, you are my elder sister,,, you should get married first,, I can't,," Nishan spoke hysterically.

"Stop speaking nonsense! You are not going to kill the fetus,,,,, its life,, dam it!,, you should have thought about this before you committed this grave mistake!" Nynisha snapped.

"But what about mom and dad,, will they agree?" Nishan was doubtful.

"They have to,, I will make them understand. Right now, you call up Prateeksha and tell her what I have advised you. Both the families can discuss about the marriage after your exams"

Nishan hugged Nynisha and wept incessantly. "Thank you sister,, thank you very much,,, I don't know what I would have done,,,,,,, without you!"

Nynisha consoled him and patted on his back and told him to relax. She went towards the kitchen. Parvathi was busy making delicacies for her family.

"Tomorrow is our anniversary,, every year Nishan surprises me with a rare gift. I wonder what he has kept in store for this year. I am waiting for tomorrow," Parvathi was delighted.

Nynisha looked withered and the thought of Nishan gave away resentful emotions. "What a plight! Mom is waiting for Nishan s gift,, and what a gift he has in store," mom would be shattered when she will learn about it!,," she stood numb in the kitchen.

"What happened, you look dull,,, Any problem?" Parvathi forestalled.

"Nothing mom,, it's just,," she stopped abruptly "let's have breakfast,, I am hungry." Nynisha didn't want to spoil her mother s anniversary.

The following day, Parvathi and her husband visited temple and prayed for their wellbeing.

The house was decorated for a small party.

Nynisha was dressed in nice blue lehanga and wore matching bangles. The party was fun with friends and relatives. Nishan couldn't face his parents. Self-condemnation was killing him.

Everybody wished the couple "Happy Anniversary" and bestowed them with a large number of gifts.

The party was over and everyone retreated. It was late in the night. Nishan had not wished them yet.

Parvathi couldn't resist and she approached Nishan.

"Where is my gift,,, Nishan?" Parvathi asked gleefully.

Nishan was back to senses. The thought of abortion had made him numb.

He had forgotten to get a gift. He felt ashamed.

"Mom the gift is,,,,, u are becoming a grandmother!" He wanted to spit it out, but his lips were locked. He didn't want to spoil her anniversary.

Parvathi looked at his mutinous face and felt a disturbance. "What happened?" she asked him softly.

Suddenly, Nynisha yelled "surprise!" and broke the silence. She had brought exotic flowers, a beautiful saree for her mother and a nice shirt for her father. She placed an envelope in their hand.

Nynisha grinned and said "this is your gift... from me and Nishan together,, please open,,,"

Parvathi opened an envelope and it contained a package tour to Goa.

Parvathi smiled but some foreboding thought struck her. Something was wrong,, something definitely wrong,, but what?,, she could not understand.

Nishan hugged his mother and said "Happy anniversary mom" he gave away a silent tear.

The following day Nynisha was busy investigating and drafting an article about a molested dead girl.

"Nynisha, you need to be safe. Avoid talking to strangers" Parvathi said imperiously.

"Mom! I am a journalist. I meet strangers every day. Our magazine publishes true stories. I want to promulgate the truth and caution people about bad circumstances." Nynisha retorted.

"I understand, but you still need to be careful." Parvathi forestalled.

"Ok mom, I will" Nynisha had to oblige.

Parvathi placed few photos on her table. "These guys are awesome. Select one" she grinned.

"Mom! This is ridiculous!,,,, I don't want to marry now." Nynisha spoke vehemently.

"You are 29 years old,,,, Nynisha!,,, I had delivered two children at your age! And you are still,,, not even married. Life is not just making fame and money. It has some meaning. How long can you be alone? You need to find love. Enjoy its bliss. You need a partner" Parvathi tried her best.

"Mom! I am getting late to office. Please,, pack my lunch. We can discuss this in the evening" Nynisha said dispiritedly.

"You can no longer escape. Make up your mind. I want your marriage to happen,,, this year!" Parvathi said gruffly.

"I cannot marry any Tom, Dick or Harry! I need to know a person. I want you to have a good caring son in law." Nynisha tried pacifying her.

"Allow me to find a groom. I will search the most perfect person for you!"

Nynisha frowned "as you wish!"

Chapter 8

T OM SAT IN HIS CAR and headed towards the exit of the
city. He saw the sign boards and he knew where his
destination was. As he drove,,,,, his childhood memories
played before him like a movie.

It was the first day of school in class V. After the summer
vacation, the kids were back. The kids discussed on only one
topic.

"You know what I did in summer?" a common question
among all.

"I went to swimming classes. Now I can swim, you know?"

"I learnt karate, I can fight. Do you want to fight
with me?"

"I went on a holiday with mom and dad to Europe!
I know you people can't afford that" a rich lad boasted
before all. The other kids envied him and hated him for his
behavior.

"Hey Tom, what did you do?"

"I went to my granny s place. I played and ate all
wonderful dishes that my granny made." Tom was happy
with what he had. He found happiness in his own world.

The bell rang and everyone assembled for morning prayers. The headmistress spoke in the mike. "Good morning children. I hope all had a wonderful summer vacation. You are stepping into a new year and a higher grade. Your performances in the exams were good. I hope all of you will continue the same. We are introducing newer methods of teaching to enable a high standard of education. All the very best for the new year ahead"

The children clapped and went to their classes. Tom sat in his class and opened his books. The first class was of mathematics and he hated it. The teacher wrote few problems on the board and asked them to solve. His pen fell to the ground. He bent to pick up and saw a pretty girl in his adjacent table. He admired her beauty.

"Who is she?" Tom whispered to his friend.

"shhh, I am solving problem!" his friend was engrossed in the book

"Who is she?" Tom was stubborn.

"She is Nynisha. New admission" his friend replied.

"Wow, she is so pretty. She is like an angel in story book" he was in trance

"Tom! Did you finish? Show me your book" the teacher came near him.

Tom panicked for a second. The page was empty. He had not solved the problem. "No Madam! I need some more time, please"

"Ok another ten minutes, then I want the answer." The teacher remarked.

Tom hurriedly took his pen and tried solving the problem. "Why don't these numbers get into my brain? Why do I feel mathematics is so difficult?"

Tom couldn't arrive at the solution and he quickly copied from his friend's book.

"Tom,, stop copying! What will you do in exam? I can't show my paper to you then" he retorted.

"I will learn by then. Now you better show or I won't give the chocolates which I have brought for you"

Tom finished and the bell rang. The following social and science periods continued and then there was a lunch break. Everyone opened their lunch boxes.

Nynisha was about to eat when her box fell to the ground dispersing all the contents it had. "Oh poor Nynisha, what will you have for lunch now?" every one asked.

Tom quickly ran and placed his box in front of her. "Have this. It's wonderful"

"No thanks" she declined.

"I brought an extra box today. My granny has sent two boxes for my friends." Tom grinned.

Nynisha hesitated a little then took the box. She ate looking at him "it's wonderful tom. Your granny is a nice cook"

"Thank you" Tom felt the happiness in his heart. His stomach made hunger sounds. He had lied that he brought two boxes. Tom couldn't concentrate in the following classes as he was hungry. But he had made a new friend.

Tom's car bumped on a stone and his car came to a sudden halt jarring his senses. Time had tapered off but it had left behind dust of memories that never settled.

"What a pretty girl, she was. I wonder where she is now" he remembered her face and slowly got off the car. It was 2 PM in the afternoon and the temperature was soaring. Tom felt the sweat dripping off is temples. The highway was deserted.

He held his hand over forehead and extended his far sight. He noticed huge Rocky Mountains on either side of road with no human creatures.

He found an old thatched hut with an old man selling cheap biscuits, tender coconut and water bottles. He dawdled a short distance and approached the hut.

"I need a water bottle and one tender coconut" Tom ordered.

The old man struggled cutting the tender coconut. Tom couldn't see his plight and he cut the coconut himself. As he sipped the water his left hand took the straw and threw it on the ground.

"Stop it!" He barked at his left hand.

The old man looked at him eerily and sat inside the shop. He gave a 500 rupees note and didn't wait for the change. The sun was getting hotter and he still had miles to go.

He started the car and pressed on the accelerator. He put on a nice music and memories again flashed across.

It was the annual day in school. Children were seen in different costumes. Tom was hesitant to participate in school events. He stood near the gate waiting for Nynisha.

After one hour she arrived in a beautiful costume of Cinderella. Tom was wonder stuck at her beauty.

"You look beautiful. You look like real Cinderella!" Tom grinned at her.

"Thank you, I had difficulty in getting this dress done so I was late"

There was an announcement and Nynisha hurried towards the stage. A small play of Cinderella was performed and Nynisha acted tactfully with grace. She received a huge applause. Tom clapped in happiness.

After the function there was prize distribution.

Nynisha adored her prize "Best all-rounder of the year"

"I have something to say" Nynisha said as she ate her ice-cream.

"Yes tell me" Tom was intrigued.

"My father got a transfer in his job and we are shifting to a new city. This is my last day in school"

Tom felt the sky falling on him. He was an introvert and hardly had any friends. Nynisha had made some difference. Now her departure would mean a total abyss for him. He cried.

"Don't cry tom. We can meet again,,, if god wants"

"If god wants? God will never want Tom to be happy" he laughed sardonically.

It was twenty years down the lane and still he never had an opportunity to meet her. "Where are you Nynisha?" he thought.

Tom arrived at his destination. He entered a small school. The school looked the same with few new modifications. He went across the corridors and classrooms. Old memories flashed before him.

He went near the playground and touched its mud. Everything was same. Nothing had changed.

He then met the Headmistress of the school.

"Hello madam. I am Tom. I studied here, twenty years ago. I have come here in search of Sulaiman"

"Sulaiman?" the teacher was confused

"The school van driver"

"These drivers keep changing. We just hire them in temporary basis and right now we do not have a driver by that name"

"Can I get his address?"

"we cannot just give away staff details to anyone who walks in here"

"It will be greatly helpful if you do so. He and my father were friends. We have some old debts to be cleared off. Please madam, do help" he looked at her and requested her intensely.

"We can check the older records and let you know."

The older files were opened and finally Tom got the address of Sulaiman. Inside, he was burning with anger.

He headed straight to the village. After searching for half an hour he finally found his house. An old lady opened the door.

"I want to meet Sulaiman" Tom looked at her.

The lady frowned at him "for what reason you want to meet the bastard. He is in jail"

"Jail?" Tom saw her quizzically.

"The bastard raped his own daughter and had made her life terrible. My poor granddaughter committed suicide because of him" the lady cried.

Tom s vengeance increased at those words. "He didn't even care for his own daughter?"

He took the address of the jail and hurried towards it. He sat in a car and worked out a plan. He made a master plan for Sulaiman to escape.

His plan worked and Sulaiman escaped from the jail. Tom offered him help and together they headed towards a mountain.

"Thank you for helping me to escape. Who are you? Why did you help me?" Sulaiman looked at him.

Tom laughed viciously. "I have some old matters which need to be fixed up"

"Old matters?"

Tom saw him with an icy glare "just stand near that tree. I will come in a moment"

Sulaiman looked puzzled but he was glad that Tom had solicited help and helped him escape. He obeyed and stood near the tree.

Tom went to the car and brought a rope. Before Sulaiman could surmise what was happening, Tom quickly manacled Sulaiman to a tree. Sulaiman resisted and twisted hard enough to escape,,, but he had become weak in the jail.

Tom took a huge rod and slashed on his skin causing deep pain on his muscle.

Sulaiman screeched in pain "what the hell are you doing? Are you out of your mind? Then why the hell you helped me to escape?"

Tom was livid and his blood boiled in retribution. He bashed him with a rod.

'this is for the sin you committed on your daughter"

Second stroke "this is for the sin you committed on me!"

Tom hit him till his hand lost power. Sulaiman stood bone weary and looked bedraggled. Then he pierced an iron rod in his anus and saw him bleed to death.

Tom sat looking at him and cried bitterly. "Because of you I have suffered every night. Now I can sleep peacefully" Tom laughed and cried hysterically.

ENEMY IS KILLED. WONDERFUL

Tom sat in his room fiddling with his diary. He leafed through the pages. His left hand unbuttoned his shirt. He looked at his left hand "why are you unbuttoning my shirt.

I am not going anywhere! I am not going to change. Do you understand? Can't you keep quite?"

His left hand slapped him on his cheeks and broke a glass of water next to him.

IDIOT,, LOOK WHO IS THE NEXT TARGET

Tom looked inside the dairy.

Chapter 9

THE SPECTACULAR FESTIVAL OF GANESH utsav which honored lord Ganesha had arrived. The festive spirits was seen in the city. The markets were full with colorful flowers, banana plantains.

Parvathi was busy in the market purchasing groceries, flowers and vegetables. The festive season brought new spirits. She finished purchasing and was about to cross the road, when a truck came speeding towards her. She froze in trepidation forestalling the accident. Siddanth jumped and dragged her to the pavement.

"Aunty, are you alright?"

Parvathi was silent for a moment. "Yes son, I would have been dead by now, if you had not saved me!"

"Relax aunty, where is your house? I will drop you."

"It's one kilometer from this market place." Parvathi mumbled.

"I will drop you safely. Pease come" Siddanth implored.

"Thank you for your help. I will catch a bus" Parvathi was in a quandary.

"I think the incident has shaken you. I will drop you safely" Siddanth finally compelled her.

"What is your name son?" Parvathi asked during the drive. "Siddanth" he said.

Siddanth dropped her near her house and turned his car to retreat. "Wait son!" she called. "You have been so helpful to me. I don't know how to thank you" she thought for a second and said "how about a coffee with this old lady? I make wonderful coffee. Please do come" she implored.

"I have to go to hospital, I will have coffee date with you some other time!" he winked.

"Hospital? But why? What happened?" Parvathi gave a quizzical look.

"I am a doctor,, and I am going for work" he smirked

"Oh doctor at my doorstep! I owe my gratefulness. Please,,, son, one coffee!" she pacified. Siddanth couldn't resist her invitation and agreed.

Nynisha was busy watering the plants when the gate opened. She saw her mother with a stranger. She approached them and took the baggage which her mom carried and she looked at Siddanth.

For the first time she felt attracted to someone.

Before she could question who he was, Parvathi spoke "this is Dr Siddanth, my savior of the day!" she introduced him gaily.

"Savior?" Nynisha frowned.

"I stood frozen when a truck was about to collide with me, but this savior has saved me today." Parvathi looked at Siddanth in gratitude.

"You just missed accident?" Nynisha was shocked to hear that.

"Relax Nynisha, I am perfectly alright. You should say thanks to him"

Nynisha shook hands with him "thank you so much for saving my mom, I am truly grateful to you"

Siddanth just replied with a smile.

He noticed the old traditional house with beautiful garden. "Your house is beautiful"

"Thank you. This is an old ancestral property which we are trying to preserve." Parvathi took him inside and made him sit in the reading room. Siddanth glanced around, there were lot of magazines and piled up newspapers and many books on journalism.

Nynisha read his mind "I am a journalist, all these books and magazines answers to your quizzical look."

"So what do you practice? I mean what is your specialization?"

"I am a psychiatrist working in 'We Care' Hospital."

"Oh that's wonderful. Actually, I had a new assignment to interview a psychiatrist and see my luck! You are right in front of me in my house!"

"Oh but I am sorry. I am already late. You can question me some other time"

"Hey I was kidding. I won't interview you now! You are my guest and the savior of my mom! Please give me your card I will take an appointment prior and then visit you. Is that ok?" she grinned.

"That would be fine" he gave his card.

Parvathi got coffee and hot pakodas from the kitchen.

"These are lovely pakodas made by my daughter. Please do have it son" Parvathi said brightly.

Siddanth ate those pakodas "hmnn really delicious. Thank you,, so much" he didn't have words to say.

"So where do you stay? And what about your parents" Parvathi was inquiring. She had liked his charm and helping nature. She dreamt of him to be her future son in law. "Nynisha and Siddanth look charming together. They make a perfect couple. I wish it comes true" she made a silent prayer in her mind.

"I stay nearby and my parents are settled in another state." Siddanth was sipping the coffee.

"Is your father a doctor too?" Parvathi went on

"No,,, He is a landlord. He has several lands and farmers to take care off".

Parvathi was in high spirits. He belongs to a rich family! He should be my son in law she thought and cackled.

"Please do keep visiting us son. Please come home for the Ganesha festival next week!" Parvathi implored.

Nynisha looked sternly at her mother. She eyed her to keep quiet. Nynisha had sensed her mother ideas. She wanted to stop her.

"Thank you for the invitation aunty. But I am going home. It's a great festival for us too. We do have a family get together. I can't miss that awesome fun. I will come home some other time." Siddanth got up to leave.

"hmnn,,,,, but son" Parvathi wanted to stop him. Nynisha looked at her mother and requested her to be quiet.

Nynisha and Parvathi stood near the door watching him leave. "I feel Siddanth should be my son in law!" Parvathi cackled.

"Mom! You just met him once and you start dreaming? You are incorrigible!" Nynisha retorted.

"Why? What's wrong? He fulfills all the criteria to be my son in law!"

"Mom! Forget it,,,,,, I am hungry let's make dinner." Nynisha walked towards kitchen.

Parvathi slouched on the sofa and dreamt of Nynisha and Siddanth getting married.

Chapter 10

ATHIRA WAS AT HOME. THE oven beeped and it was time to take out the cake.

"Wow! It looks delicious mom!" Rohan tried grabbing the cake. "Wait honey it's hot!" Athira resisted.

"I want it now" he was cribbing. Athira retorted "learn to have patience,, my boy!"

Rohan played with the utensils and suddenly peeped through the window. "Mom, what's that?" he pointed.

Athira peered through the window and noticed blood stains in her neighbor compound.

She visited the old couple anxiously and knocked the door. Indira opened dispiritedly.

"There are blood stains in your back yard. I just saw through the window!" Athira spoke vehemently.

"Blood stains? How could it be? Let's see" Indira took Athira to the back yard. It was a horrific scene and Athira felt sick.

An animal was chopped into pieces.

"I think it's the work of some animal" Indira was succinct in her expression.

"Animal? Which animal can come here? This is a residential area?" Athira was retorting.

"hnnn,,,, may be a dog has hunted its cat" Indira spoke airily.

"May be" Athira said hesitantly. But, she felt something was definitely odd.

Athira retreated home. She heard prayers, chanting and hymns. "Something is fishy,,, I feel odd about this old couple,, something is not right" she thought and began her work.

The following days appeared more mysterious. She found beheaded dead animals in her backyard.

She constantly heard hymns,, chanting mantras and Her nostrils often felt the perfume of incense sticks.

One day, Athira saw a goat in backyard.

"Indira aunty, what is goat doing in backyard?"

"One of our village friends had come. They gifted this goat to have a scrumptious lunch. Do you like mutton biryani?" Indira looked at the goat maliciously.

"No thanks" Athira said grumpily and hurried towards her house.

The following day, Athira witnessed a gory scene of animal sacrifice. She puked in vexation.

Such horror incidents often confronted Athira. She was a pure vegetarian and the sight of dead goat, disgusted her.

She wondered how people could kill the animals. She always wanted to promulgate to the world

"Be vegetarian! It's good for you" and she often wrote articles pursuing them.

The summer vacation was on and Rohan spent his time in streets and play ground. The kids enjoyed playing cricket, badminton and outdoor games. The hot afternoons were reserved for video games.

"Rohan,, it's time for the lunch! Come soon,," Athira yelled. Rohan was with his friend immersed in a video game.

"Rohan! Come for lunch." Athira yelled again. She waited for half an hour but he didn't return. Athira surmised that he must be completely immersed in his videogame. She visited his friend's house.

"Rohan, come for lunch!" Athira screamed.

Rohan s friend came out "he is not here,, he left half an hour back. He said he will have lunch and return, our video game is still pending, we are in the last level" he chuckled.

"He left half an hour before? But where is he? He is not back still. Did he go somewhere else?" Athira was getting tensed.

"No aunt,, he said, he was going back home."

Athira s instincts said "something is wrong"

Athira swiftly retreated home to have a check, but Rohan was not there. She trotted entire colony in search of him,, but,,,, he was no where

Her anticipation increased and she immediately called her husband.

"Rohan is missing,,, I don't know what to do,,, please come home fast,," she wept incessantly.

"What are you saying? How could you be so careless? Check with his friends and neighbors, I will be there as soon as possible" her husband cut the phone.

Athira squirmed on a chair. Her heart was filled with despair and she was losing her sanity.

She called Nynisha "my son is missing,,, I have no idea, where is he" she sobbed.

"What? Don't cry,,, he will be fine,, just be strong,,, I am coming" Nynisha pacified her.

Nynisha arrived and couldn't see her plight. She enveloped Athira in her arms and consoled her.

"I want Rohan,, my son!" Athira wept.

"Stop crying,, please,,, did you check everywhere?"

"Yes,,, he is missing! I am afraid,, what if he is in trouble?"

"I will check,, please,, control yourself" Nynisha pacified her and walked out.

Suddenly, Nynisha heard chants, temple bells and some hymns from the neighbor house. She peeped through the window and saw an old couple performing some sacred pooja to goddess kali.

She also noticed something strange. There were knives, hammers and other butchering instruments before the idol.

Nynisha sensed danger at the freaky sight. She peeped more through the window.

She was baffled to see Rohan.

He was manacled on a wooden board and he was unconscious. They had nailed him mercilessly. There were strokes of burns on Rohan s abdomen.

Nynisha s instincts made her run to the backdoor. Luckily it was open. She barged in and startled the couple.

"What the hell are you doing?" Nynisha expostulated.

The old couple was frightened for a second.

Suddenly, Indira took a sword in her hand. "Don't you dare move,,,, I will smite Rohan s head before you. This is a sacred sacrifice, I can't let it go"

Nynisha feared at the moment. She had to save Rohan. She had to act fast.

She quickly looked around and found a vase with flowers. Without a second thought, she threw it on Indira s face.

The vase hit Indira and she lost balance. Nynisha pounced on her and tried grabbing the sword. She and Indira fought stubbornly with their strength. The two ladies rolled on the ground and struggled with each other.

The old man looked on petrified and suddenly took a stick and held it up in trajectory. He was about to hit Nynisha when Athira attacked him from behind.

Athira pushed the old man on the ground and fixed him up with her strength. Her eyes burned in anger and her muscles tightened in vexation. She slapped the old man.

The old couple couldn't fight any more and breathed heavily.

Nynisha and Athira manacled them to a chair.

Athira slapped Indira and glowered "How could you? I saw you as my mother! But, you turned out to be a sinister witch! Rohan adored you and what have you done to him"

Nynisha slapped this time "why did you do this?"

Indira was struggling to breathe and she slowly muttered "I was numb, when the doctors told me that, I have a brain tumor. I won't live long; I was plunged into worry and depression. I felt hopelessness. I wanted to live. The doctors had given up hope.

I decided to make a religious tour and spend my last days in harmony with gods and devotion.

It was then, I met a tantric. He enlightened me that, if I sacrifice a child, I can attain the child's life. I can live long. I was lured away by what he said.

I had to sacrifice a child and propitiate the deity, only then, my wish will come true.

I decided, the child would be Rohan. I waited for an auspicious day and it was today. But,,, you interrupted!"

Athira and Nynisha looked on unbelievingly.

The superstitious beliefs have lured people since centuries. They didn't except to come across one.

Athira added in vexation "you are just evil and nothing else. No wonder, god punished you with brain tumor. I wish, you die this very moment. How could you kill an innocent boy for some depraved belief?

You have sacrificed animals too. I should have been more cautious and investigated before. Whenever I smelled aromatic perfumes and chanting of hymns, I felt odd. My instincts, always said,,,,

Something was definitely wrong.

I wish I had confronted you before. I still shiver at the thought of my son getting sacrificed.

I had sensed trouble before. But, I never knew, my neighbors are my worst enemies! You have to pay for this" she slapped her hard.

Nynisha swiftly called an ambulance and police.

Athira took Rohan to the hospital. Nynisha helped the police in arresting the couple.

The news spread like a forest fire and people barged in vexation. They wanted the couple to be stoned to death. The police controlled the mob and they were taken to the custody.

Chapter 11

Tom put on the jogging clothes and slouched at the shoe rack. He picked up a pair of white shoe. His left hand took off the shoes from his right hand and placed it back in the rack. It picked up another pair of shoes.

Tom looked at his left hand sardonically "what is your problem? You disagree with whatever I do?"

His left hand slapped him again. Tom was distraught and he put on the shoes and went for jogging. He arrived at a local park and saw the morning joggers.

He noticed a group of people laughing out loud for no reason. He asked a jogger "why are they laughing?"

"Its laughing club" the jogger replied.

"What?"

"It's kind of cardio work out. You get more oxygen and you feel energetic. It also helps in healing certain illnesses like hypertension, depression, headache and many more"

"Can we get rid of depression?"

"I think it will reduce to great extent" the jogger grinned

Tom decided to experiment and joined the people in their laughter. He knew none of them but still enjoyed being one among them for a moment. He laughed out loud till he felt rejuvenated.

The irony of life had made Tom to have only a psychotic laughter.

For that moment he really felt calm and serene.

He reached home and he heard his master voice

YOU CAN LAUGH AFTER THE TARGET IS COMPLETE

His left hand took his pocket diary and leafed opened the pages.

TARGET 1 and 2 executed

Target 3 pending

He opened his diary and looked at his next target. He dialed a number in his cell phone "where is he? Did you find him?" Tom asked sternly.

Tom s lips curled in happiness as he got some news.

Tom cut the call "I have to wait for another 4 days! Let me work up a plan" he scribbled few notes in diary and closed it.

Tom went to the study room where his father was busy calculating the year end income tax.

"Dad,,, I am feeling depressed. Can we go out for a holiday?"

His father frowned "the year is ending and we have major issues of income tax. I am too busy. Sorry son. Enjoy with your friends"

Tom expected the answer and retreated to his room.

Idiot why are you calling your father? You are not going out for a holiday. You have mission to accomplish.

Jayanth had recently married Jigna and he was taking her to Andaman Island for honeymoon. Jayanth had decided to travel in ship. It was a three day journey and they wanted to enjoy the sea.

Tom had received information and he booked a ticket.

Enjoy your last days Jayanth. I am coming

The ship debarked from the port and entered the sea. A photographer stood at the entrance of the ship, ready to snap the picture of the passengers. The ladies stood posing in front of the camera with their windblown hair, faded make up and wrinkled clothing. "Madam this is your before cruise picture" he smiled at the ladies.

The photographer approached Tom; he simply denied and boarded the ship. He reached the cabin with the help of an escort. He unpacked his luggage and took the map of the ship to explore.

The ship was huge. It was like a city on the sea. It rocked and rocked and people had to get adjusted to it. It sailed into the sea entering into the tranquility of peace. Only water was visible to the farthest sight.

The first day was interesting for Tom. He was excited at the sunset and the mystery colors that played in the sky. The orange ball sank increasing his anxiety.

The night was amazing with the twinkling stars in the sky. The ship glittered with all its lights. He ordered the sea food and enjoyed the scrumptious meal. A cool breeze swept giving a soothing effect to his mind body and soul.

Tom couldn't sleep that night as his mind reckoned the plan and the ways to execute them. The second day in the ship was getting more fun. Tom swam for hours in swimming pool and felt refreshing. He slept on a lazy chair, bathing in the sun. His left hand pulled out the diary and threw it before him.

"Can't you keep quite?" he cursed his left hand. His hand was behaving weirder day after day. "I need to consult a doctor" he thought.

SHUT UP DON'T GO TO THE DOCTOR. HE CAN KILL YOUR MASTER

Tom heard the loud voice of his master and he felt, he should always obey him.

Tom evasively looked at the sky and his eyes shut at the scorching rays. He wanted to be alone.

The cruise suddenly stopped and people began to panic. "What happened? Why did the ship stop?" everyone questioned.

An announcement revealed that a boy had jumped off the deck. The cruise won't move till they find him.

"I hope they will find the man soon or this ship won't move"

IF THE SHIP DOESNT MOVE THE MISSION WILL BE DELAYED! DAMN IT!

The ship stood still for few hours and finally they found the boy.

The ship began to sail again heading towards Andaman.

It was last day in the ship. Tom sat on the deck gazing at the orange sky. The sun glittered elating the mood of the observers.

Jayanth stood holding the railing and viewed the sky. Tom looked at Jayanth like a poisonous snake. He just wanted him dead. His left hand wanted to strangulate him. Tom neared him but saw a lady approaching him. He quickly retreated and covered his face with a hat.

Jigna embraced Jayanth and kissed him. "I have never seen such a beautiful sky! It's wonderful. I am elated about her honeymoon."

"It's just the beginning sweet heart!" Jayanth kissed her passionately. Tom was irked at the sight. He couldn't bear their romance and retreated to his cabin.

"He cannot be happy, I will take off the happiness from him,,,, for the sin he has committed he needs to be punished!"

Tom opened his diary and made a sketch.

The ship finally landed at Andaman and people disembarked. The tourist team leader took them to hotels. They were asked to rest for some time and then proceed exploring the beautiful flora and fauna. The lush green canopy soothed the spirits. There were plenty of water sports and tourists thronged to explore.

Jayanth and Jigna hired a honeymoon suite. The room was extraordinary with modern amenities, Italian Jacuzzi. The view from the balcony was splendid.

Tom followed Jayanth and booked a room adjacent to his.

The night was the last night for Jayanth and Jigna to make love. They crawled on the bed exploring each other and celebrated their honeymoon.

The next morning Jayanth woke up with the calling bell sound. He lazily dawdled and opened the door. "Good morning sir, here is your morning tea and a note"

"Note?"

"Your wife gave"

A surprise for you near scuba diving, come soon,, waiting for you.

Tom had bribed a waiter and had delivered that note. He had noticed Jigna going for morning stroll and he quickly started his plan.

"I like surprises honey! I am coming" Jayanth hurried towards the water sport.

He met the diving instructor.

"Did my wife come? Where is she? Is she in sea?" Jayanth asked in curiosity.

"Two batches have already gone in sir. I don't know who your wife was!" he grinned

"Well,,,, give me the equipments, I want to plunge in too" Jayanth smiled.

"Is this your first time? Shall I give instructions?"

"Not required, I have done it many times. Just give me the apparatus" Jayanth put on the dry suit and swiftly dived into the sea.

"She must be exploring the ocean,, I am coming honey!". Jayanth thought

The sea always mesmerized with its unique beauty. It was a different world with complete peace and silence. A school of fish, corals urchins, giant cucumbers, octopuses welcomed him.

He proceeded further and tried to catch up the team.

Suddenly, he felt difficulty in breathing. He tried hard to breathe in and out with his mouth, but oxygen was lacking. He slowly realized that his oxygen tank was almost empty. He was startled and made a rapid uncontrolled ascent to the surface and suffered a fatal air embolism.

Tom grinned viciously as he noticed Jayanth losing his life. Tom had emptied the oxygen tank before Jayanth entered for scuba diving.

Tom ascended high celebrating the death of Jayanth.

Target 3 killed

Early in the morning Jigna went on for a morning stroll. She had asked Jayanth to accompany her, but he lazily slept off. Suddenly something hit her head and she collapsed on the ground.

When she gained conscious she was blurred. Then she noticed something on her hand.

Somebody had written "you are free from that bastard. Go,,,, live your life" she couldn't understand what it meant.

Tom sat on the shore and looked at the wilderness. He uttered a cry of joy. The past had withered him, but he had to be strong to complete the task. The loneliness crumbled him. He had no reason to live.

He had to plan for his next target.

Chapter 12

SIDDANTH WAS IN HIS CLINIC reviewing his patient's records. The intercom buzzed and he picked up "Hello"

"Good morning Dr Siddanth. Miss Nynisha wants to meet you. She says she has taken an appointment over the phone." The receptionist spoke.

"Yes, send her in" he placed the receiver.

The door opened and Nynisha entered his cabin. "Good morning Dr Siddanth"

"Good morning Miss Nynisha, please sit down. So what can I do for you?"

"I am writing an article on alcoholism and its deaddiction. I need your help."

"Sure, I will help you. Alcoholism is a social stigma and people should know about the deaddiction. You are doing a good job."

"Thank you. Why do people get addicted to alcohol?" Nynisha started her interview.

"It is a kind of substance use disorder which can affect anyone. There is no exact cause for it but partly it does depend on genetics- biological traits. A person's environment, psychological traits, and stress level also play major roles."

"What are the symptoms of this addiction?"

"One of the most important signs of addiction is continued use of alcohol despite experiencing the serious negative consequences of heavy alcohol use"

"Can people get rid of this dependence?"

"Yes, they can. There are many centers for deaddiction. Usually it is one month residential treatment program. Psychological therapy is also required to make lifestyle changes"

"Does family play any role?"

"Yes of course! If the head of the family is a chronic drunkard, you can imagine what effect he can have to the entire family. Family involvement and counseling is an integral part of the treatment plan. The family members need to communicate with each other and discuss openly about their feelings."

"The society accepts the male drinking and male chauvinism. There is a sheer open imbalance and people treat women alcoholics as an outcast. This prejudiced bias is incorrigible. Do you have deaddiction unit for women?"

"It's sad to know about this bias in this society. But irrespective of gender, age or socioeconomic status, I strongly believe that every person has a right for professional treatment. We have a separate ward for female patients in the deaddiction unit and we exclusively cater them for their needs to overcome the dependence."

"Thank you so much to enlighten me about this regime. You can see this interview in our next month edition."

"You are welcome. I hope this will help people"

"I am twice grateful to you, for saving my mom and helping me with this article" Nynisha grinned.

Nynisha was about to leave when suddenly she remembered something.

"Sorry to trouble you again. I need some more help. I have a new assistant by name Falak. I have observed a strange behavior in her. She often takes excuse from me and visits bathroom to wash her hands. She always complains that, her hands are dirty and she is afraid of those million germs. Her hands are always clean. We work in a journal office and everything is kept clean. Something is wrong with her"

"It's one of the commonest forms of OCD."

"OCD?" Nynisha looked at him quizzically.

"Obsessive compulsive disorder. Here the obsession is of contamination with dirt or germs and the compulsion is washing of hands repeatedly many times a day. It becomes ritual for them.

It's a psychiatric condition where an idea intrudes into the conscious awareness repeatedly. It is recognized as irrational and absurd. The patient tries to resist against it but is unable to do so"

"Oh,,, is it that bad?"

"No,, it can be treated,, we can do psychotherapy, behavior therapy and advise some drugs"

"That would be great! Shall I call her in?"

"Yes, sure."

Nynisha brought Falak inside.

Siddanth noticed anxiety in her face.

"No need to worry. I can help you in every way. Tell me what's troubling you" Siddanth grinned at Falak.

Falak spoke "thank you so much for offering help. I got engaged two weeks back and my fiancée has a problem with me. He doesn't like me washing hands"

"Falak, it is common to go back to kitchen to check whether the gas is turned off or not. Or to see iron is unplugged or not, but if you are suffering from obsessive thoughts and compulsive behaviors, it will affect your daily life."

"Yes, I have a thought in my mind that my hands are contaminated with germs. I wash them regularly till my hands wear off. I have tried controlling but I feel I am helpless."

"You have an elaborate cleaning ritual, but this obsessive thought becomes stronger. This compulsive behavior ends up with anxiety and become more demanding. These compulsions can consume your life to the point of social isolation."

"Doctor,,, is there a solution for this problem? My fiancée has warned me. If I don't get rid off by this, then I may lose him" Falak sobbed.

"Relax Falak. There is a solution and it is cognitive behavioral therapy. First of all, you need to say, my hands are not dirty, it's just my obsession that they are dirty. I need not wash my hands. They are clean. You have to repeatedly say this in your mind or you can write it down in a paper.

The second step is to refocus your attention. When you experience this thought and urge, shift your attention to something else. For example, you can start walking, listen to music, start knitting or play a game in your mobile phone. You have to do this at least for 15 minutes in order to delay your thought and urge.

At the end of delaying period, sit and reassess your urge. I am sure the intensity of the urge would have subsided. Then start delaying even longer. The longer you delay the urge, the more it will likely change."

"Whenever I am stressed, I feel like washing more. What to do then?"

"The stress often makes the obsessive compulsive behavior worse. At that time, you sit and meditate or do yoga or deep breathing. You have to practice relaxation technique for at least 30 minutes a day. You can also do aerobics which boosts your mental energy by releasing endorphins."

"Thank you so much Dr Siddanth. I am really grateful to you. I didn't know it's a kind of disease I possess. I should thank Nynisha too for bringing me here."

"You can attend our sessions, I am sure you will get relief from this."

"Thank you, Dr Siddanth for your help. I appreciate your gratefulness."

"You are welcome"

Nynisha and Falak headed to office to complete their work.

Nynisha reached home and switched on her computer. Parvathi kept a photo on her table.

"Look at this!" Parvathi grinned.

Nynisha looked in surprise "Dr Siddanth s photo?"

"I got it from our marriage broker. He is of our same caste! His parents are finding a suitable bride for her. And you can be his perfect bride!"

"Mom! I am in no mood to marry!"

"No more excuses! We have fixed an appointment with his parents this weekend. You are supposed to be here. Do you understand?"

"Mom, I have an important conference to attend I cannot be here."

"Your marriage is my first priority. I don't care about your conferences and meeting. I will tell them to come home on Sunday. Sunday is holiday and you ought to be here!"

"Sunday! No way. I have to cover important project."

"Nynisha! Be here on Sunday. This is final" Parvathi walked off.

"How can they insist what they want? I am mature enough to decide what I need!" Nynisha was annoyed.

Chapter 13

NYNISHA S PARENTS WERE BUSY MAKING arrangements. Siddanth s family was visiting them. Parvathi was anxious. She hurried across, to set things straight.

India is a land of diversity and Arrange marriage is still a norm. Though love marriages have evolved in recent years, people still opt for arrange marriages. A marriage completely depends on human compatibility and thinking. As a tradition, two families interact with each other to look for similar interests and nature.

It was evening. The house was beautifully decorated. Aromatic incense sticks rejuvenated the environment. The place was pleasant.

Nynisha looked charming and elegant. Parvathi had nervous jitters playing in her stomach.

Nynisha brooded over "is he the right one?" she was anxious of that new stage in her life.

Parvathi hugged her "I hope the meeting goes on well and you will like him"

Their talk was halted when they heard a car honking.

"They are here! All,,, be ready." Parvathi was insisting everyone in the house to be on their toes.

Siddanth s family arrived.

Parvathi and her family welcomed them with a Namaste.

"You have a nice house!" Siddanth mother Laksmi commented.

"Thank you so much." Parvathi cheered.

The families introduced each other. Siddanth was getting bored among the busy conversation of the oldies. Parvathi noticed him "I think it's time for the boy and girl to meet. I will get her in two minutes"

Parvathi hurried towards the room and escorted Nynisha to the living room.

Siddanth had met Nynisha in two different occasions. This was the third meeting and it was completely different.

Nynisha walked in and all eyes focused on her. She wore a simple pink saree with minimal jewelry. Her simplicity, honesty and her charismatic attire adorned him.

Nynisha did Namaste and touched his parent's feet. It was a common tradition in India where children touch the feet of elders in due respect and seek blessings.

Laksmi asked Nynisha to sit beside her "you are the prettiest lady I have ever met. I like your simplicity and your long hair. You are charismatic and my son will be lucky, if he marries you. I hope, you guys end up in marriage. You two make a wonderful couple" Laksmi grinned.

Nynisha thanked Lakshmi for her compliments.

Parvathi cut in "I think Siddanth and Nynisha should have a private talk" she guided them upstairs and led them to a balcony.

Siddanth and Nynisha stood facing each other.

"I feel this meeting is odd!" Nynisha spoke first.

"So you don't want to have an arrange marriage?" Siddanth looked at her quizzically.

"I didn't mean that. I feel, we both could have met and discussed in prior and then this family meeting traditions customs should have been. We need to know each other before we make a final decision"

"I respect my parent's words and I know you too. So we are standing here in balcony looking at each other quizzically. I just want to be honest. I am a doctor and I spend lot of time dealing with patients. I may not come home early or often take you out often. You are working lady and I hope you can understand."

"I appreciate your honesty Dr Siddanth. It is a busy and competitive world and everyone have to do their best to reach the top. May be together we can plan and make our life better."

"Yes, I agree. This is not the first time we are meeting. It is the third time and we are already acquainted with each other. So I hope there is no anxiety or hesitance. If you have any questions you are free to ask." He grinned.

"I want to thank you again for your help and information regarding deaddiction of alcohol. It's getting printed. You can see it in next edition."

"That's good! Looking forward to it" he smiled

"Ok shall we join the family talking then?" she looked at him.

"Yes, I have something more to say"

Nynisha cocked a brow "I am hearing"

"You are beautiful,," he wobbled.

Nynisha cackled "thank you. I thought you were of geek stereotype! You do appreciate things around. Nice to know that"

Nynisha and Siddanth were back in living room. "I hope the conversation went on well. I hope the answer is yes from both of you?" Laksmi saw him inquiringly.

"We need time to think and then proceed" Siddanth looked at Nynisha.

"I agree making decision isn't easy. Take time and think about it. We oldies will be happy if the result is positive" Laksmi grinned.

"It's time for dinner,, shall we move towards the dining table?" Parvathi invited them.

The dinner had wonderful delicacies. The families enjoyed each other company.

"Looking forward to see you again!" Parvathi cheered.

"Definitely. I am sure this match will click." Laksmi and Siddanth waved bye and left.

Parvathi and Nynisha cleaned the vessels and the house. Nynisha was on bed reading a book. Parvathi approached her.

"So how was the evening? What did you talk in the balcony? I hope you didn't give him negative thoughts!" Parvathi asked her anxiously.

"Mom! I know you are very anxious about my decision and all I can say is,,,,, he is a nice guy."

Parvathi was exalted "That means it's a yes! Wow,, I wanted to hear that. I will call Laksmi now!"

"Mom! Cool down its eleven o clock in the night. You can talk to her tomorrow. Have patience!"

Parvathi couldn't sleep that night as she was really excited. Her only aim was to see their marriage. She waited for the sun to peep out again.

The following morning she hastily prepared breakfast. Nynisha came to the kitchen. "Mom! Don't be so anxious, everything will be fine."

"What if they reject our proposal? I can't handle rejection" Parvathi jittered.

"Mom,,,, take it easy. It's no big deal if they reject" Nynisha was casual.

"How can you be so casual? Don't you like him?" Parvathi frowned.

"Like him? I don't know what to say. He is a good person. I still don't have feelings for him" she gulped the toast and omelet.

"I just pray that my dream would come true" Parvathi sat on chair and sipped the coffee. "Oh my god what a bad coffee is this. I am not able to concentrate on my work"

"Mom! You will miss the school bus. Hurry up! Your kids are waiting for you." Nynisha kissed her mother and left to office.

Parvathi packed her lunch box and hurried towards the door. She put the key in lock when she heard the phone ringing.

"Is it a call from Lakshmi?" she pushed the door and hurried towards the phone. She picked up and said "hello"

"Hello is it Parvathi?"

"Yes,,, may I know who this is?"

"I am Laksmi, Siddanth mother. Are you busy?

Parvathi looked at the clock. She was already late for the school. But she didn't want to miss this important call.

"Not at all" she smiled genially.

"We like your daughter very much. Siddanth said yes to the proposal. I just called to inform you. We would like to know your answer."

Parvathi felt as if she was sailing in the clouds in heaven. Thank god! She looked at lord Ganesha.

"It's a yes from our side too!" she proclaimed cheerfully.

"Oh that's good news to hear. Then we shall meet next Sunday and decide about the marriage date and ceremonies."

"Oh that's wonderful" Parvathi was jubilant

"I invite your family for dinner. Please come home and we all shall discuss together"

"Definitely" Parvathi said in high spirits.

Parvathi let out a cry of joy. Her dream was coming true.

Nynisha was in her office busy editing reports. Athira joined her for a quick gossip.

"So how was your weekend?" Nynisha asked her.

"As usual, went to a mall, did shopping and helped Rohan in play stations. What about you?"

"Siddanth s family visited our home with marriage proposal"

"Oh really! Unbelievable,,,,,,,,,, Finally, you have agreed for marriage. That's great. So what happened? Any progress?" Athira asked her in high spirits.

"I think I am getting married,,,,,,,,,," Nynisha said in a dulcet tone.

Athira hugged Nynisha "congratulations! I still can't believe it"

"Thank you"

"Promise me that you will take me for all the shopping. You know that I am a shopping freak! Wow! Shopping those wedding sarees, jewelry, accessories etc,,, I am already ready!" Athira was galumphing.

"Hey,,,,,,,,,, it's my marriage,,,,,,,,,, not yours! I will definitely take you along. Who else can select the best for me?" Nynisha grinned.

Jisha came hurrying to the cabin. "Boss is calling you"

"I can't tolerate this old man and his tantrums. His only wish is to torture the employees!"

Nynisha hurried with a file.

Chapter 14

A NEW LIFE WAS WELCOMING HER. Nynisha had mixed feelings of nervousness and happiness. She was intimidated to know how Siddanth felt.

Nynisha and her mother were in a car. Parvathi spoke "I can see smirk on your face. I know you are excited in this new relationship"

"Mom!,,,,,, Actually I feel it like a mystery. I need time to open up the layers"

"I am sure it will blossom over time into a perfect one and Siddanth would be your perfect partner" Parvathi grinned.

Lakshmi had invited Nynisha and her family to discuss about the wedlock.

They arrived at Siddanth s house. It was a beautiful villa nestled midst landscaped gardens. It was just serene.

"What a beautiful villa!" Parvathi was exhilarated. "I am really happy for you" Parvathi eyed at Nynisha.

"Welcome to your new home sweetheart. I hope you like it" Laksmi hugged Nynisha and welcomed her.

"It's beautiful. I loved it" Nynisha grinned.

Laksmi was excited to show her villa but Nynisha s eyes were busy searching Siddanth.

"We just brought this villa two months ago. It has open plan area with living room which has direct access to the pool in the garden. The inside dining area has modular fully equipped kitchen and top quality fixtures. And you must see the first floor which has Jacuzzi bath and gym equipments,,,,,," Laksmi was blabbering with her endless talk.

Parvathi marveled at the luxury as she saw many things for the first time.

"This villa is incomplete without a pretty lady like you. I am really waiting to show my friends that I have a prettiest daughter in law" Laksmi cackled and suddenly jabbed her head "I forgot to tell you about the priest. He may be coming any moment. Let's go to the living room"

The priest arrived.

"Welcome Punditji,,, We were waiting for you. I hope you are not tired in this scorching heat. These are the horoscopes of Siddanth and Nynisha. Kindly look at them and give us dates for an engagement ceremony and marriage." Laksmi placed them on the table.

The priest viewed the horoscopes scrupulously and finally said "the couple will be blessed if they exchange rings on an auspicious day and I suggest next Wednesday will do good"

"Impossible! How can I invite my friends and family in such a short time? And what about shopping? Jewelry?" Lakshmi was fretting.

Parvathi spoke in "relax Laksmi. Don't fret. Together we can make it happen."

The priest was immersed in the horoscope.

"Any problem, Punditji?" Laksmi was anxious.

"Not at all. You are lucky to have such an amazing daughter in law. She is having a wonderful zodiac sign"

"That's great news. I just want the couple to have a happy married life." Lakshmi cheered.

"Punditji,,, what about the marriage date?"

"I suggest next month"

The ongoing talks of pundit and Laksmi were never ending and Nynisha was getting bored. She abruptly broke their conversation. "Sorry to disturb you aunt Laksmi, but where is Siddanth?"

"Oh dear! I forgot to mention. He was called for an urgent meeting in hospital. He may come late. Why don't you search for some literature or novels in his room? He has a great collection" Laksmi responded.

Nynisha agreed and set foot exploring the magnificent bungalow. She traipsed on the long spiral staircase and proceeded up. The villa had several rooms and Nynisha had difficulty in finding the exact one. At last she found a room with a big bookrack. She slowly scrutinized the books.

"Laksmi aunt is right. Siddanth has a great collection"

A photo album in the upper rack caught her eye. She was intrigued to see. She quickly pulled it out and flipped open. The album was a collection of photos of childhood to present. Nynisha smiled as she saw each photo.

She sat mesmerized in the time travel of photos. Siddanth was adorable as a baby, and then she saw him in school uniform, his tantrums, his plays, prizes and his friends.

When she had finished screening something caught her eye. The last few photos depicted moments of togetherness with a girl.

She flipped opened the album again from first. It was photos of college days. Siddanth and a girl were together in most of the photos.

Her stomach lurched in nervousness "is she his girl friend? Why did they break up? Why didn't Siddanth tell me? Why I am fretting? Everyone has a past. I should look into the future,, but,,, I am not able to digest these photos,,, who is she?"

She was apprehensive.

Nynisha tried to calm down, but restlessness, vexed her.

"Nynisha,,, it's getting late. Come down." Parvathi called her from beneath.

Nynisha climbed down the stairs. "How is Siddanth s room? Did you find anything interesting?" Laksmi grinned.

"Yes many interesting things" Nynisha mocked a smile and thought about the girl.

Lakshmi had arranged a scrumptious lunch. "We will do our shopping on Sunday. I hope Nynisha is free" she spoke to Parvathi.

Nynisha received a call from her office. She had to get back to work.

"Your home is truly beautiful and thanks for the wonderful lunch. Will see you soon, I need to go now" Nynisha gave a warm hug to Laksmi.

Nynisha dropped her mom back to home and headed towards her office. She got stuck in traffic and she was losing patience. She looked around for passages where she could squeeze her car and pass through but there was no way.

She jabbed her head in frustration and looked around. Something caught her eye. She saw Siddanth with a girl in coffee shop. Nynisha pursed her lips "is this the same girl, the one in the photo? And what is he doing in coffee shop? He was supposed to be in an urgent meeting in hospital. Is this a meeting? Lakshmi aunt lied? Or Siddanth lied?" several questions perturbed her mind.

Her cell phone rang jarring her senses. It was Jisha calling.

"Hello"

"Boss is angry"

"Why?"

"You are late again and you haven't submitted the reports he had asked for"

"That bonehead can wait" Nynisha gave a heavy sigh in agitation.

"This bonehead can't wait. You may be fired"

Nynisha was vexed "I don't care" and she slammed her phone.

The traffic cleared and the other cars honked in frustration. Nynisha quickly glanced at coffee shop to have a second look, but they had vanished.

The cars still honked irritating her further.

"Ok I am moving" she drove the car further and reached office.

She rushed upstairs and quickly met Jisha.

"How is the jackass?"

"Very much vexed at you"

"That's bad" Nynisha frowned, but she had to face him. She reached his cabin and knocked the door.

"Come in" she heard a grunting voice.

"Good afternoon sir, here are the reports, you had asked for"

"I don't need your reports!" he said indignantly.

Nynisha had to tackle the moody boss and she decided to be polite and pacify him "I am really sorry sir, I was stuck in traffic"

"I don't want your silly explanations" he resented.

Nynisha knew that confronting the irritable boss is a difficult task, she decided to stay calm. "I am sorry" she pleaded again.

"Your recent work hours are very bad and you end up submitting reports lately. This is press. Damn it. We have to be quick! Your tardiness can ruin us. I don't need an imbecile employee like you. You are fired, now leave" he piqued.

Nynisha stood frozen for a second as she couldn't comprehend his words. "You can't fire me. I am one of the best employees. I apologize for my recent tardiness but you know my reports are up to the mark and nobody can question them" she retorted.

"I am the boss! I decide what to do. It's over. Just leave" he was determined.

Nynisha walked off from his cabin with tears in her eyes. Feelings of dejection and frustration played along. She slowly walked to her cabin and packed her things.

Athira came running "I saw your ill fated face. What happened?"

Nynisha muttered "he fired me"

"What? Come again!"

"Yes, you heard it right! He fired me" she howled.

Athira was shocked to hear that. She would be missing her best friend. "Boss is irritated since morning, but how could he do that? His mood swings are getting varied these days. I am sure he will call you back. Keep watching" she tried pacifying her.

"I have sea of opportunities. I can't tolerate this snappy jackass anymore. To hell with him!" Nynisha walked off in vexation.

Athira stared helplessly.

Nynisha drove her car with quandary of thoughts. "What a day! My engagement got fixed in the morning. Afternoon, I saw Siddanth with another woman. Evening, I lost my job!" she laughed heartlessly.

Nynisha reached home. She dropped her things on the couch and silently walked towards her room.

Parvathi jubilantly made scrumptious delicacies. She was happy about Nynisha s engagement and wedlock. She saw Nynisha going to her room

"Dinner is ready,,,,,," she called everyone fondly.

Nishan saw the wonderful dishes "wow mom! Lovely"

"Let's celebrate the happy occasion" Parvathi grinned.

Nynisha sat facing her family with a melancholic smile. Having mixed feelings of happiness and sadness was something unusual and awful.

Parvathi sensed something wrong "what's the matter my child?"

Nynisha didn't know how to reveal the matter.

"I can see,,, something is bothering you"

Nynisha had to let it out "my boss fired me" she muttered.

The family was distressed for a moment and together they rebuked "what?"

Parvathi hugged her "I can't believe it,,,, but why? You are such a workaholic,,, what made your boss say that?"

"The savvy boss has lost his mind" Nynisha said flatly

"Do not worry my dear. To lose and gain is a part of life. When a door closes another will open, but you need to have patience and wait for the right time"

Nynisha couldn't control and she let out her tears. She needed the family at that moment and they were present to support her.

The dishes on the table looked at them questioningly.

Nishan decided to break the sadness "chill buddy,,,,, lets cheer for the happy part and forget the worst. I am sure your moody boss will call you morning. Now let's have dinner,,,,,,,,, I can't miss it" he grinned.

Late in the night, Nynisha was about to sleep when the cell phone rang. Siddanth was calling. She bluntly cut the call. His lie had vexed her and losing her job had made her even more agitated.

The phone rang again.

She sighed heavily and switched off the phone.

Nynisha awoke when the sun rays hit the window panes and the flowers danced in the sunlight. The brightened flowers were proclaiming a renewal of optimism.

Her mom broke in "someone is waiting for you"

Nynisha indolently asked "who mom?"

"Come, see for yourself" Parvathi grinned.

Nynisha dawdled towards the living room and was surprised to see Siddanth.

"Good morning!" he gave a bright smile.

Nynisha looked at him quizzically and said "good morning"

"Let's go for a walk" he said.

"Walk?"

"Is it wrong to walk with my fiancé?" he smirked.

"We are not yet engaged" she snapped.

"We will" he pulled her hand and took along. Nynisha was reluctant but she gave in.

For a short distance, they walked in absolute silence, and then Siddanth broke in "I am sorry. I couldn't make it yesterday"

Nynisha looked at him 'you lied' she thought.

"I had an important meeting"

Nynisha stopped him "stop lying"

Siddanth looked at her in bewilderment "lie?"

"You lied to your mom that you were attending an important meeting, but I saw you with a lady in coffee shop" she rebuked.

As a psychiatrist he was good in tackling things and he quickly understood the scenario.

"Now, I understand the cause of your anger. I can explain,,,, if you have patience"

Nynisha had lost her temper but still pretended to be calm "ok go on"

"What time did you see me in coffee shop?"

"Why are you questioning me? I am supposed to ask. Who was that woman? Why you didn't come? Why you lied?" she cocked her brow.

"Relax! What time did you see me in coffee shop?"

Nynisha puffed and said "3 PM when I was stuck in traffic"

Siddanth spoke "I didn't lie to my mom. It's just a slight misunderstanding. I had taken a day off to welcome you and your family. I was suddenly called for a meeting and I had to rush. After the meeting I was driving back home, when my mother called up and said that you had already left. I felt bad for not meeting you. I decided to make it up in the evening, but something else came up"

Nynisha snapped again "the lady in coffee shop!"

"Relax! My dear,,, the lady in the coffee shop is not my girl friend. She was Prisha, my best friend. We are family friends and our parents are business partners. She is a doctor too. And for your kind information she is a married woman. She had come up with some urgent problems and I had to deal it"

Nynisha was embarrassed at her imbecile act. "I am really sorry, I was mistaken,,,, it was not my day at all" she frowned.

"No need to be sorry. It happens. I can understand what you underwent yesterday. Losing a job is awful. Remember,,,,, nothing lasts long. Good time will come" he smiled.

"You know that I lost my job?" she felt abashed

"Your mom told me. I can understand what you are going through,,, but,,, please be optimistic,, don't lose hope" he grinned

A greater Coucal flew above them. Nynisha exclaimed "did you see that?"

"What?" he remarked.

"A greater Coucal! It's a good omen" she grinned.

"You mean to say, all other birds deliver bad omen?" he laughed.

She smiled faintly "it's just a belief. My mom keeps telling. It gives a feel of optimism"

"Good,,,,,, be optimistic" he held her hand for the first time and caressed it. Nynisha was taken aback but she felt good. A romantic spark was just glittering.

The cell phone rang breaking their romance. George was calling. Nynisha didn't want to speak to that bonehead after the horrible ordeal and his snappy remarks.

Siddanth pacified her "you just felt optimistic and you saw greater Coucal. Go on,,,,,,,,,, pick up the call"

Nynisha hesitantly picked the call and said "hello"

"Good morning Nynisha. I am sorry for what happened yesterday. I was upset and I vented out my frustration on you. I can't believe myself,,, I fired you. You said it right,, you are one of the best employee I have, I apologize again. Come back" George slowly muttered.

Nynisha didn't want to risk again but Siddanth whispered in her ears "say yes"

Nynisha grinned and said "ok sir"

"Then come quickly, I have loads of work to hand over" he guffawed.

Nynisha cheered "I am coming"

Chapter 15

———◆═◆◆═◆———

THE EVENING BREEZE WAS PLEASANT and the garden was still and cool. The garden was lit up with colorful lights and beautiful flowers. A pleasant aroma welcomed the guests.

It was the engagement day of Nynisha and Siddanth.

Nynisha walked graciously towards the stage in her beautiful attire of a perfect golden lehenga and pearl jewelry. Siddanth was mesmerized at her beauty and met her gaze as she walked forward. He slowly whispered "you look beautiful". Nynisha could feel her stomach fluttering. A new relation was beginning.

Her heart quivered as he held her hand. The priest asked "are you ready for the promise?"

Siddanth smiled "yes"

"Then, go on,,,,,,,,, exchange the rings. It's a perfect time" the priest said.

Siddanth looked into her eyes and she could feel the love and affection. He slowly slid the ring into her finger. Her heart leapt as she felt the connection.

It was her turn and she quickly slid the ring into his finger. The families cheered in happiness.

Parvathi blessed them "now, you are wearing the fitting symbol of wedding promise. This ring marks the beginning of journey filled with wonder, surprises and tears. I wish for all the happiness"

A soft music was played and they were asked to dance.

Siddanth wrapped his arm around her waist and the couple slowly danced to the soft tune. People cheered them and blessed them.

Nynisha could feel the romantic sparks emitting from his eyes and she hid her face in shyness.

Parvathi heard a commotion outside and she walked fast to see the matter. A bunch of eunuchs were trying to barge in. Parvathi quickly knew why they had come for.

"Let us in, we are here to bless the couple"

Parvathi snapped "we don't need your blessings"

"Beware! We can curse them" a eunuch yelled.

Laksmi walked in and threw away a bunch of notes "take this money and move out. I don't want any more disturbances"

"This is not enough" a eunuch cried.

"Shall we call the police?" Laksmi rebuked.

The eunuchs decided to move off and dispersed.

Lakshmi patted on Parvathi s shoulder. "Relax this is common here. They just need some money"

Parvathi was vexed but pretended to be calm.

The function was coming to an end and everybody gathered for a family portrait. It was time to retreat and Parvathi packed her things. She collected the gifts and cards.

Siddanth caught Nynisha in dressing room and kissed her. "This is not allowed!" she sniggered.

"Why not? You are my fiancée now" he grinned.

Nynisha wanted to kiss him back when she heard her mom calling "it's getting late dear. Come quick"

"I will see you in café tomorrow" She winked a smile.

"But the kiss is still pending" he held her tight.

"This kiss can wait" she tantalized.

"No!"

Nynisha couldn't resist and kissed him passionately on his lips. Siddanth was longing more when she quickly released herself.

"Keep dreaming" she smiled and waved a bye.

Nynisha was back in the office and the staff encircled her to congratulate. She thanked them and moved to her cabin. A bunch of envelopes were waiting for her to be opened. She scrutinized each of them and segregated them. A black colored envelope caught her eye. It was something unusual.

She quickly opened and saw a piece of paper with a few words.

I hope you liked the gift!

"Gift? Which one" she thought.

Jisha came running "boss is calling"

Nynisha hurried towards his cabin.

"Congratulations Nynisha!"

"Thank you,, Sir. I expected you to come" she smiled.

"Sorry about that, I was held up in some urgent tasks. I will not miss your marriage" he grinned. "A circus company has just arrived in town. They want to advertize through our magazine. Meet them and brief up. You can make a small article about them"

"Sure sir"

Nynisha retreated home and she was flooded with cards and gifts. She relaxed and opened one by one. A black box caught her eye. "Why am I seeing only black things today? A black envelope on my office desk and now this black box. Is Halloween coming up?"

She slowly opened the box and was baffled. It contained a bouquet of black paper roses.

"Black paper roses? What the hell?" she eyed at them in irritation. A small piece of paper popped out and she unfolded it.

Beginning of black doom

"What nonsense? What doom?" she was intrigued.

Her cell phone rang.

"Hello Siddanth"

"You sound dull. What happened?"

"Someone,,,, is playing pranks. I received a black box with black paper roses"

"What? I have received a black box too, but I didn't get time to open it. Hold on, will check and let you know"

Siddanth opened the box and his eyes turned red in anger. It contained a bunch of nude photos of Nynisha.

He picked the phone and said "your nude photos"

Nynisha couldn't digest for a moment "what?" she yelled.

"This cannot be a prank. These photos are morphed ones. Someone,,, playing hard. We have to find that bastard. We will inform the police"

"I will hang the bastard myself." Nynisha said indignantly.

"Tomorrow morning we shall meet near police station?"

"I have an assignment of interviewing circus people. I will come there after that"

"Don't worry honey,, we will find the bastard" Siddanth cut the phone

Chapter 16

THE CIRCUS WAS IN OUTSKIRTS of the city limits. Nynisha drove to the circus and a black sedan followed her. She reached the circus and put on her identity card. She decided to view the show before she interviewed them. The show was at 10 AM and she waited eagerly still lingering on her thoughts.

She leafed through the pamphlet. The first act was of an acrobat. The circular dome looked stunning with colorful lights and the stage shimmered with brilliance.

The acrobats made a grand entry in bicycles and climbed the rope to teach the top. Their movements were elegant, almost natural and indeed they came from years of practice. The act received applauses and enthusiastic cheering.

It was followed by a bike stunt, tiger act and clowns entertaining the crowd. Nynisha was getting late and decided to interview fast.

She met the manager "hello, I am Nynisha from 'Verity' magazine. You had approached our magazine for an advertisement. Here are the lists of documents we want. And I need a quick interview with your team, so that we can publish it well"

The manager was pleased to help "Meet Milan, the acrobat you just saw."

"Hi Milan, you were fantastic, I appreciate your talent. So what made you an acrobat?"

"I come from a poor family who struggles to keep the ends. I was mesmerized by these acrobats when I had seen them for the first time. It was difficult to convince my family as my life is always on risk. But here I am performing in front of the crowd. Initially, I was apprehensive. Now I can soar up in the skies" she grinned.

Nynisha met another junior artist. "Don't you miss your family?"

"I do miss sometimes. This team is good and they take good care of me" he smiled

Nynisha spoke "this life is not easy. You put on lengthy hours of practice to perfect your acts. But what if you fall sick? Then how will the show go on?"

"We grow up and believe that we have to be really sick not to work. We need power and we gain it by practicing every other day. It is not just the talent that we empower but our will to work continuously to reach our goals."

"So how long these artists can perform? Is there any age limit?"

"No age limit. It varies from individual to individual. Some perform till 30 or 40 years. Then they chose to be only coaches and help in administrative work" the manager curled his lips

Nynisha winded up the interview and thanked the team for their great help. She walked towards her car fidgeting with her cell phone.

"I am already late,,, Siddanth must be waiting. I need to hurry" she thought.

In a far corner a man put on the clothes of a clown and disguised himself. He took out a sharp knife and examined it.

Ready to kill he thought.

He slowly approached her. Nynisha was busy in her phone and did not notice the clown. The clown neared her and was about to stab her when he heard someone yelling from behind. He withdrew and retreated in vengeance.

The circus manager was hurrying towards her. "You had left your purse in my office" he handed over.

Nynisha gratefully thanked him and started her car. Her cell phone rang and it was Athira.

Nynisha picked up "Hello Athira"

"I am stuck up in hospital" Athira cried.

"Hospital? What happened?"

"I had fever and chills in morning. I visited hospital and doctor diagnosed it as malaria."

"Poor Athira,,, I will come soon" Nynisha consoled her.

"Can you do me a favor,,,, please pick up Rohan from school"

"Sure, take care"

Nynisha had to change her plans "I can visit police later; I have to catch up with Rohan. Athira is sick. She needs me" she thought.

Nynisha started the engine and pressed on the accelerator. The road was deserted. She had miles to go to reach the city. She just checked in rear view mirror.

A truck was behind her.

She put on a soft music and zoomed in.

Suddenly she noticed the truck was speeding towards. Nynisha quickly pressed the accelerator and increased her speed.

She saw a clown driving the truck.

"Who the hell is he?" she quivered.

The speedy truck followed her quick. Nynisha panicked, shivered and increased her speed. She was driving at the maximum limit.

The truck just rammed the car and she lost the balance. She hit the pavement breaking the wall of the bridge.

The next moment Nynisha was seen crushing down into the river below.

Shiver ran down her spine as she felt she was meeting her death. The car plunged into the river entering deep down towards the river bed. She struggled to open the door. Water surrounded her and she could rarely breathe.

This is my last moment in life.

She saw her family and her beloved Siddanth in a glimpse. Tears welled up but were washed away by water. She could feel water entering her lungs.

She was dying.

Suddenly a man opened the car door and grabbed her hand. He pulled her out and swiftly swam towards the shore holding her.

He reached fast and made her lie on the ground. She lay unconscious before him.

He quickly placed his heal of his hand on her chest and gave compressions. Then he gave breaths in between and rescued her.

Nynisha regained conscious and coughed out water.

"You are fine, relax!" he blurted.

Nynisha lay motionless for a moment. The sudden accident had baffled her. She had miraculously escaped death. The thought of her car pounding into the river made her to tremble. Cautiously she lifted herself and sat resting her back against a tree.

She looked at the stranger and said "thanks!"

"I saw the speedy truck hitting close to you. You were off in the air hitting the river. I jumped at that instant to save you."

"Thanks again. Someone was trying to kill me. He was a clown. I saw him in rear view mirror" Nynisha slowly muttered.

"He tried to kill you? Who is he?"

"I have no idea" she frowned.

"Let's get out of here. He may come again, looking for you. Can you walk or shall I carry you?"

"I can walk"

The two slowly walked towards the highway. "I will drop you home" he said.

Nynisha immediately remembered that she had to catch up with Rohan. But she was not in condition to visit the school.

"I need to make an urgent call" she said.

"I don't have a cell phone. There is a coffee shop nearby, you can call"

"Good, let's hurry"

He drove his car and they approached the coffee shop. Nynisha quickly called Athira "sorry Athira I had a minor accident. Cannot pick up Rohan"

Athira was shocked. "Accident again? How are you? Where are you?"

"Relax Athira,,, I am fine,,,, we shall talk about this later. You pick up Rohan"

"Sure take care"

Nynisha cut the call and was feeling week.

"Shall we have some coffee and sandwiches?" he asked.

She nodded and they sat on couch.

"Your name?" he asked her sipping coffee.

"Nynisha" she grinned.

"Nynisha!,,,,,,,,," suddenly old memories flashed in his mind "did you study in 'Saint Mary' school in Bagalkot?" he asked enthusiastically.

"Yes, but how did you guess,,,?" she saw him quizzically.

"We studied together! Guess who I am?" his face lit up in surprise like a small boy.

"You mean,,,,,,,,,,, we were batch mates?" Nynisha asked in surprise.

"Of course "he smiled.

Several faces passed against her eyes, like a computer checking for the match.

"Sorry, my mind is blocked a bit, not able to remember" Nynisha jabbed her head.

"I am Tom. I had given my lunch box, when you had dropped yours"

"Tom! Is it really you? You look different with bald head" she smiled.

"You looked beautiful in that Cinderella dress. I cannot forget those days" he laughed.

They conversed for a long time on their nostalgic memories.

The night crept in and a chilly breeze made Nynisha shiver.

"Take this,,, put on" he handed his coat to her. She refused for a moment, but the cold made her to take.

"How did you land up like a messiah and saved me?"

"God sent me" he grinned.

Tom s left hand was fidgeting with a fork. He tried to control.

"What happened?" She looked at him puzzled.

"Nothing,,,,,,,, my left hand doesn't obey me"

"What?" she exclaimed.

"It sounds freaky,, but its true"

"Consult a doc,, it may help. Well,,,,,,,, it's getting late. I have to leave. My fiancée would be worried"

"You got engaged? Congratulations!,,,,,,, when is the marriage?"

"Next week,, do come" she smiled

"I will" Tom gave her a friendly hug and they parted.

Siddanth winded up his work and looked at his watch. It was eleven PM. "why hasn't Nynisha called yet. The circus is far off city. She should have been back by evening" he sat worried. He tried calling her cell phone, but it always said,,,, the phone is unreachable.

He heard a knock on the door and he slowly opened. Nynisha hugged him and cried.

Siddanth was taken aback by her sudden presence. "What happened? Why are you crying?"

"I miraculously escaped death today"

"What?" Siddanth babbled with his mouth hung open.

"I was returning from the circus when a truck rammed at my car. My car flew in the air and I landed up in river. My hope was ebbing when suddenly Tom rescued me. He came in like a messiah."

Siddanth couldn't comprehend what Nynisha was talking. She explained slowly.

We have to meet the police right now.

Siddanth and Nynisha arrived at police station. It was late in the night and constables had dozed off.

Nynisha patted on a constable shoulder "we want to meet the inspector"

The constable pointed a cabin. Nynisha and Siddanth entered his cabin.

"Sir we have a problem"

"Yes go,,, on" the inspector drawled.

"I just escaped death today. I was driving my car in city outskirts and a truck rammed my car"

"So you want to lodge a complaint on the truck driver? Did you notice the truck number? We can track down"

"It wasn't accident,,,, he wanted to kill me" she said in apprehension.

"What makes you thinks so?" he said curtly.

"Clowns don't drive a truck" she sneered.

"Clown?"

"I saw him in rear view mirror. He was wearing a dress of a clown"

"So you suspect someone from circus?"

"Not exactly,,,, I had received a strange gift recently. A Bouquet of black paper roses and it had a note 'beginning of black doom'. My fiancée also received a black box but it contained nude photos of mine. We had planned to lodge a complaint in the morning. But,,,, I ended up close to death" she was panting.

"This sounds like a mystery, any suspects you think of?"

"I have no idea" Nynisha pondered.

"You can lodge a FIR, we will try our best" the officer said

Nynisha wrote the complaint and retreated home. She was panicky and week. She rested her head on his shoulder "don't tell this to mom,, she will be disturbed"

"Sure" Siddanth assured her and kissed her gently. "Take care, see you tomorrow" he dropped her home.

Chapter 17

THE FARM HOUSE WAS WELL illuminated with dazzling lights. People were moving around in their drunken state. A lavish party was organized by Sahil. His friends were having a blast.

Tom parked his car just outside the farm house to have a close look.

Next target, he smiled. He kept a close watch on his activities.

Sahil swayed in euphoria as his girlfriends flocked around him, caressing him and trusting their eyes upon him. He was inebriated in alcohol and was losing his balance.

The party was fun with boys and girls. They danced and grinded against each other.

"Do you like games?" he asked his friends.

"Yes" they uttered together.

"Then,,,, let's have fun" he yelled in exhilaration. "How many ready for car race?" he queried his friends.

A girl stopped them "you guys are drunk,, it's not safe,,, don't go" she said.

Sahil brushed her off "it's my party,,, I do, what I want,,, no one can stop me" he said arrogantly

Sahil and his friends zoomed out with cars. Sahil floored the accelerator and he took off in a boom. He hated losing. He increased his speed moving ahead of others. It was mid night and the roads were deserted.

Tom followed the cars, and he wanted to knock him down as soon as possible. This is the right time he thought.

After several twists and turns the cars zoomed across a hilly terrain. Suddenly, Tom heard a loud thud and he stopped.

Sahil s car had rammed to a tree and he lay unconscious on the steering wheel. Tom neared him and his heart burned in anger. He came close and felt his nostrils. Sahil was still breathing.

Still not dead!

Tom turned crimson and his left hand tried strangulating him. But, he had to stop suddenly. He heard Sahil s friends coming in. Tom tried to pull out his hand, but his left hand was stubborn. With great difficulty he released his hand.

Sahil s friends came rushing in "what happened?" they were shouting.

Tom said "your friend is unconscious, he needs to be hospitalized. But you guys are drunk; you may land up with police. I can help you out"

Sahil s friends agreed and they went to hospital with help of Tom.

"The bastard is missing out!,,, I wish, I could have finished him tonight" Tom tightened his fist in frustration and anger.

Tom helped him in hospital and then retreated home. He was restless and fidgeted with his phone. His heard his master s voice

You need to hurry

Tom had to do something.

Two days later, Sahil had recovered and he went out for jogging. Tom followed him.

As Sahil was trotting, he suddenly stumbled and fell. He cried in pain as his ankle was twisted.

Tom rushed towards him and his killing instincts wanted to strangulate Sahil. But, he had to control his vexation as joggers were around.

"What happened? Do you need help?' Tom offered his hand.

Sahil clutched his ankle and let out a cry.

"Looks like sprain. Will help you to hospital" Tom said hesitantly.

Sahil nodded and Tom took him to his car. He made Sahil comfortably sit in front seat and he began to drive.

"Thanks buddy,,, I owe you this" Sahil smiled. "Your face looks familiar. Have we met before?" he asked intriguingly.

Tom replied curtly "I helped you out,,, two days ago, when you rammed a tree and was unconscious. I had taken you to hospital"

"Was it you? Then I owe you twice" he guffawed.

"Yes,,, you owe me lot of things,, I will retrieve it, when time comes" Tom smirked.

Tom dropped Sahil in hospital "I need to go,, I have some work" he said.

Sahil gave him a friendly hug "we will meet again,, thanks"

A week later

The turf club was busy with the crowd and people thronged the paddock fence trying to view the parading horses. They looked on in anxiety and were deciding which horse to bet on.

The jockeys came out fully dressed with saddles and mounted on horses.

Sahil was a club member and he didn't have problem in getting his seat. He put on his expensive sunglasses and looked on. He was grinning as he had made the best bet.

He was startled when someone patted his back. He looked behind and it was Tom.

Sahil was happy to see him and he quickly gave him a friendly hug. "You,, a club member?"

"Yes" Tom replied.

"So,,, have you placed your bet?"

"Yes,, number 5"

"You should have placed on 7. That jockey is fantastic" Sahil bragged

"Is it? Let's see" Tom mocked a smile.

The bell rang and the gates were opened. The horses took off in thunder. They galloped in full speed and the jockeys struggled towards the finish line. The crowd cheered on their bet horses.

Sahil and Tom looked on in anxiety.

The race was over in a minute, and number 5 had won. Sahil felt a lump in his throat as he had lost quite a sum of money.

Tom was excited to see his wretched look. "It's ok buddy,,, it happens" he tried cheering him up.

Tom was grief stricken and he had pledged to avenge him. He wanted to punish him with impunity. And he waited for a right time. Tom had become his friend sheepishly. Sahil couldn't surmise his vicious will.

Tom smiled at the thought of his immolation.

Sahil prided himself in his luxury and his parties were never ending. Sahil gave Tom a flight ticket. Tom looked at it intriguingly.

"My birthday buddy,,, lets rock and roll. I have booked a resort in a beautiful country. Pack your bags" Sahil called him amiably.

Tom irked at his sight but he kept his control. "Time to end" he thought.

The gang landed into a lavish resort surrounded by pristine beach and exotic nature. The myriad of fountains and crystal chandeliers welcomed them.

Sahil s girlfriends converged on him and kissed him. They were excited on that rendezvous party.

"This is fantastic!" Sahil was exhilarated.

The hotel staff offered him drinks "Sir, we have a good casino. If you are interested, we will be happy to help you" a manager said.

"Sure, I will plan in the evening" he said.

It was dusk. Sahil and his friends thronged into the casino. The casino was captivating with slot machines, table games, poker tables and slot wheels whirling.

"I like roulette,, let's play" Sahil bragged.

He placed his chips on few numbers and the dealer spun the ball. The ball swirled and came to a halt. It was not his number and Sahil looked on gloomily.

A cocktail waitress swarm across to cheer him up and offered him martini. Tom patted on his shoulder and whispered 14.

"You want me to bet on it?" he asked

"Yes" Tom smirked.

Sahil placed his chips on the number and looked edgily at the roulette. The dealer spun again and the ball swirled halting at number 14.

Sahil was gratified and he quickly gave Tom a warm hug. "I am lucky to have you" he smiled.

Tom grinned sheepishly and thought "you haven't the slightest idea of what foreordains you"

"I want more martinis" he said. Sahil was getting intoxicated and it favored Tom to execute his act.

After playing for a while, Tom whispered in his ears. "It's getting late, we need to go"

Sahil was sober and he gazed his eyes over slightly and rolled his eyeballs a bit "I want to play more" he said in a relaxed tone.

"We need to go" Tom gave a sinister look. Sahil got up and fell on his arms. Tom supported him on his shoulders and walked out of casino. He took him to the deserted beach.

Sahil was blabbering in his intoxication and he was losing his balance. He didn't have the slight inkling of what awaited him.

Thud,, Sahil fell on the sand.

Hurry his master was saying

Tom strangulated him in aggravation till Sahil took his last breath. Sahil couldn't resist in his inebriated condition and he gave a slight groan. He was stone dead.

Tom looked at him in awe and he laughed at his triumph.

Chapter 18

———◆◆◆———

SIDDANTH AWOKE ENTHUSIASTICALLY. HE HAD a reason to be happy and why not,,,,,,,, it was his wedding day. He was going to wed his new love,,,, Nynisha.

It was a typical south Indian wedding with plethora of traditions, each symbolic of beautiful and noble sentiments. The walls were hung with jasmine garlands and its sweet fragrance made it a place of delight.

Full grown plantain trees were tied to both gateposts; festoons of mango leaves and marigold flowers, a bright rangoli and the notes of nadaswaram, the south Indian shehnai welcomed the guests.

Siddanth was dressed in a silk dhoti with golden zari and an angavastram. His attire accentuated his style and personality.

Siddanth was brought in a procession from a temple in flower adorned ride. The bride s parents escorted him to the marriage mandapam.

Lord Ganesha was invoked, to keep away all the hindrances.

Lakshmi walked in with an umbrella, a fan, walking stick and a towel containing dhal and rice. "Now the best part begins" she laughed.

"Mom, what have you brought? Don't expect me to carry all of these"

"Dear son, you are going for kasiyatra" she sniggered.

"I thought I was going to wedding hall for my marriage,,, but,,, you are sending me to pilgrimage?"

Everyone laughed and the priest spoke "son,,, this is a mock pilgrimage. You have to pursue further religious studies and renounce worldly pursuits"

"No way,,, I am already a doctor,,, have completed my higher studies,, and I am waiting to marry Nynisha" Siddanth frowned.

"This is just a tradition and its fun,,, just go on" Laksmi smiled.

"Ok,,, I am renouncing everything and heading to a pilgrimage" Siddanth was walking out. Nynisha s father intervened "wait,,,,,,, don't go,, married life is superior than ascetic life,, I promise to give my daughter to you as a companion"

Siddanth laughed "truly?,,, I will quit going,, take me fast,, I want to see Nynisha" he guffawed.

Nynisha looked like a goddess in a beautiful silk saree and artistic golden jewelry. She had plated her long hair with flowers and beads. She was the cynosure of all the eyes. She walked graciously towards the mandapam. Siddanth was awestruck by her beauty.

The parents solemnized the final betrothal ceremony as the vedic priests chanted the appropriate hymns.

Siddanth and Nynisha sat on wooden planks. "You are gorgeous,, feel like kissing you right here" Siddanth whispered in her ears and gave a naughty smile.

Nynisha hid her face in shyness.

The priest proclaimed "exchange your garlands and symbolize unification"

"Now it's time to tie the knots of mangalasutra,, Siddanth are you ready?" the priest asked.

"I am ever ready" he was exhilarated. He gently placed the mangalasutra on her neck and tied the auspicious knots.

"Is this marriage ceremony over, can I and my wife go for honeymoon now?" he sniggered.

"You ought to have patience,,,,,,,, son, still rituals are pending" the priest smiled.

Siddanth was feeling the rituals were tedious and never ending "why can't they just leave us,, I am losing patience,, come let's elope" he hushed.

Nynisha tantalized "patience sweetheart"

"Now,, the vital part of wedding. Hold the bride hand and walk with her seven steps" the priest said.

"Only seven steps? I want to walk with her till my last breath" he let out a heavy sigh.

"By walking seven steps you will become good friends and remain inseparable"

"That's great!" Siddanth quickly held her hand "together we will walk and live for eternity" he whispered.

The ceremony ended and Siddanth and Nynisha were now husband and wife.

Parvathi and her husband blessed her "be the queen in your husband's house and glorify yourself with good nature and virtues and be in good conduct with your mother in law"

It was evening and it was time to relax and rejoice. The family gathered and ladies sang poking fun at the bride and groom. Nynisha allured him with a song and Siddanth looked on mesmerized.

Between all the relatives, customs and chaos, Siddanth and Nynisha were encircled with a pyramid of gifts. They were completely exhausted with the long hours of standing and innumerable photo sessions.

Siddanth wanted to just collapse on the bed when his friends joined him. "You look tired; spare some energy for first night. Eat this ladoo" his friend winked and forced a ladoo in his mouth. Siddanth s friends poked him and guffawed tactlessly.

It was time for Nynisha to bid farewell and proceed to Siddanth s house.

Parvathi looked on, mingled with emotions of pathos and joy. Daughters are a true treasure and it is disappointing to depart from them. She remembered her first touch, when she held the new born baby, her first crawling, her first walking and falling, her mischief and every other moment she had spent with her daughter.

Nynisha and Siddanth arrived home. Friends and relatives flocked around teasing endlessly. Lakshmi came to their rescue "give them privacy!"

She took them to the room and locked the door. The room was decorated with flowers and incense sticks. Siddanth was nervous and at the same time exhilarated.

It was their first wedding night.

Siddanth neared her and she sucked in a deep breath. The anxiety and nervousness made her to have goose bumps on her skin.

Her heart raced wildly and she could feel the same emotion sparking in him.

"I was waiting for this moment" he said and looked into her dark brown eyes. He could feel the burning desire and passion. His soft touch electrified her as he wrapped his arm around in a tight embrace.

Love blossomed as they explored each other.

The next morning Laksmi knocked the door. Siddanth opened and saw his mom with coffee mugs. She placed it on a table and squeezed his ears mischievously. "Did you sleep?" she smirked

"Mom!' he let out a shrill and smiled.

"Pack your bags and run,,, here is your honeymoon tickets." She tossed it on his hand.

Siddanth looked at the tickets "wow! So this was the surprise you talked about" he hugged her.

"Kind of,, now get going, before your friends barge in again for all the nuisance questions of first wedding night" Laksmi giggled.

Nynisha and Siddanth packed their bags and arrived at airport. They saw the board. The plane was delayed. They sat in the waiting room discussing about the previous night.

"So how was it?" He tantalized.

"What?" she winked

"First wedding night!" he smiled mischievously.

"Hmm good" she said.

"Just good? The word is fantastic!" he laughed.

An announcement was made and they went to take their boarding pass.

The plane took off and they sat in the plane waiting to land on an island.

The organizer welcomed them and escorted them to a speed boat which took them to a small exclusive coral island which was ringed by beach. The resort boasted itself of tranquility and had lush green vegetation with beach villas.

"This is a perfect honeymoon getaway. We have classic villas with private pools, exuberating natural elegance" the organizer boasted.

"You should try this fruity mock tail,, it's just amazing" he offered them two glasses.

Nynisha saw sundecks with loungers, easy chairs and ladders leading to a lagoon. She sat on the chair relaxing and touched the golden sands. Her hands rejoiced with those fine particles giving a titillating experience.

She looked at the spectacular turquoise lagoon and lost into tranquility.

"If you want any information regarding sightseeing and beach sports, please do contact us. Enjoy the island and have a pleasant stay" he greeted them and left.

Siddanth quickly closed the door with "Do not disturb" card. He looked at her naughtily.

"Let's get started sweetheart! Did you see the Jacuzzi? I am dying to make love" he was about to undress when Nynisha pushed him and opened the door. She quickly ran towards the lagoon.

"You can't escape,, I am coming" Siddanth caught her and they rolled on the sand playfully.

Nynisha had found her love. A loving husband any girl would ask for. They played and made love on the sand.

In the evening they visited the thatched parasols of beach bar. The sun went down and the live bands, DJs, energetic dance floor became the center of activity.

They sipped cool cocktails and margaritas and danced enjoying the DJ. The delectable island had traditional cuisine which was mainly based on coconut and fish was truly cherishing.

Exploring the blissful coral reefs with bright fishes was fun. They visited scintillating islands with golden silver sands and enjoyed the water sports, Snorkeling, surfing, parasailing and wind surfing. The water sports were never ending and they enjoyed it to very extent.

It was early in the morning when Nynisha awoke. She saw her lovely husband sleeping peacefully. She cupped her hands on his chin and kissed him sweetly.

"I love you" she whispered.

"Me toooo,,," he drawled in sleep.

"You wanna go for a walk? It's amazing outside"

"Walk in the evening sweetheart, now just make love,,," he smiled.

She pushed him mischievously "I am going for a walk. You keep dreaming"

Nynisha put on jogging pants and went for a stroll. The pristine beach beckoned her and she strolled barefoot experiencing the sand. Tiny crabs tickled her foot and she giggled.

She was mesmerized and lost in the tranquility when someone pushed her down. She fell with her face hitting on the sand. A man pounced on her and held her tight. She wrestled and kicked him throwing him in water.

Her instincts made her run. She ran as fast as she could, but it was difficult on sand. The man rushed behind her and caught her. She tried to escape but in vain. He dragged her and tied her up to a coconut tree.

"Stay away bastard!" she screeched and tried escaping the knots.

"Not so easy,," he laughed maliciously.

"Who the hell are you? What do you want?" she scowled at him.

"Revenge!,, He looked at her with scornful eyes.

"Revenge?" Nynisha looked at him confusingly.

He slowly took out a knife and sharpened it on a stone. "Do you have any last wish?" he said sheepishly.

Nynisha wanted to buy time. She knew Siddanth would come looking for her "why do you want to kill me?"

"A long story" he laughed. "Fine, if that's your last wish, then listen,,, Do you remember Shyam? The pharmaceutical owner"

Nynisha s mind was perturbed and she was fidgeting. "Who the hell is Shyam?" she thought and suddenly it dawned on her.

A few months ago, Nynisha was assigned to interview a local orphanage. She wanted to help them in collecting funds. She visited the orphanage and opened the gates. She saw children running around. A few were in play area. As she looked, smile radiated from them. A sense of happiness engulfed her.

She met an old lady who was the care taker of the children.

"Good morning Nanny, you sure have provided a good place for these kids to grow up."

The old lady smirked "I have tried my best to bring smiles on these tiny faces. I just wish some funds will pour in and make their lives even better"

"Let's pray that your wish will be granted. I will help through our magazine. I am sure there are people with good hearts who will be willing to help. Can I look around and talk to children?" Nynisha pacified her.

"Sure" she smiled.

Nynisha moved around to see the play area, the kitchen, and dormitory. She spoke to few children and they seemed happy in their own world. She went to rooms for a check and she saw a little girl shivering with high fever.

Nynisha touched her and she was burning hot. She immediately drove to a local hospital with the girl. The doctors examined and made some tests.

"She is suffering from malaria. We need to treat her quick"

"Go on,, doctor. I will pay the bills" Nynisha said. Nynisha felt pity for the child as she had no one to take care. She decided to stay with her.

The child was given anti malarial drugs, but she showed no improvement. The child entered into coma.

Nynisha panicked "what's wrong doctor? Why has she gone into coma?"

"Sorry to say,,, she has developed cerebral malaria, she is sinking,, she may die"

"What? No,,, it can't happen,,, do something doc,,, please save her" Nynisha was petrified.

"We are trying our best, she is not responding to treatment,,, sorry Nynisha" the doctor said sadly.

She hugged the small girl and cried, but the child lost her life. Nynisha couldn't stand it. She didn't know how to reveal it to the old lady. The unbearable sadness crumbled her.

A few days later

Nynisha was driving towards a village on an assignment. Her spirits rose as she passed through lush green paddy fields and lake. The undulating roads led to a small village. She had to pass a small valley. The place was deserted as it was bright sunny hot. The field workers had gone for rest.

The tires were not pulling and she stopped her car to check. She stepped out of car and saw a punctured tire.

"Gosh! I need to change the tire now!" she jabbed her head. She placed her hand over forehead and searched for some help. The hot afternoon made her drip with sweat.

At the far end she noticed a truck. It had parked next to a small hill. "The truck man could help me" she thought.

She trotted towards the truck and when she came closer, she noticed there were two trucks. They were exchanging some boxes.

Nynisha felt odd for a second.

"Why are they exchanging boxes in a deserted area? Something is fishy" she sighed.

She hid herself near a tree and opened her camera. She tried zooming in and focused on the men.

The men appeared panicked and were working fast. The exchange was complete. A man offered a brief case. The other man opened and his faced smirked as he saw money.

One truck left

The man sat behind counting the notes. He was jubilant with the stashed money.

Nynisha looked around and found a log of wood. She neared him and smote him from back. The man fell unconscious. She pulled him up and manacled him to a tree.

She got inside the truck and opened the boxes. They were loaded with medicines. "Why are they exchanging medicines? What does this contain? Cocaine?" questions swirled in her mind.

She caught a water bottle and then ran towards the man. She poured water on him and he slowly gained conscious.

"What are you dealing?" she scowled at him

"It's none of your business" the man muttered.

Nynisha banged him with a rod. "Tell!" she shouted.

He screeched in pain and slowly said "fake drugs".

"Fake drugs? What do you mean?"

"I replace the original medicines with duplicate ones" he slowly said.

"You deal with fake drugs and play around with people's lives?" she spat on him and smote again.

He cried "stop"

Nynisha dialed for police. There was no network in her cell phone. She looked around for help. She saw some villagers heading towards fields. She yelled for help. They looked at her and came running.

She quickly revealed what had happened. The villagers were vexed and stoned him. Then they took him to a police station.

The hot afternoon and the incident had drained her. She collapsed on the ground and closed her eyes. She was feeling uneasy and saw a vision. The child was dying before her and she looked on helplessly. The doctor was saying she is not responding to treatment,,, we have given the medicines

Then it dawned on her. "Only if,,, the child had original medicines,, she would have been alive,, she would have been playing,," she cried in grief.

The pharmaceutical owner was caught and was taken for a trial. He was jailed. He was convicted for making counterfeit drugs.

The company was closed and he was behind bars.

Nynisha came back to reality. She was tied up to the coconut tree and was in dismay. She came back to her senses "that bastard should have been sentenced to death. How could he kill people with fake drugs?"

"Shut up! I don't care about people. All I care is,,,, only about Shyam. You fixed him up. It was all because of you,, he is in prison." He glowered.

Nynisha looked around "where are you Siddanth,,, come fast,,, save me from this psychopath" she prayed.

"Why do you want to kill me? And,, why do you care about Shyam?" Nynisha wanted to buy more time and she kept on questioning him.

"He was my friend, my love, my everything and I am missing him"

"Love? Are you gay?" she laughed.

He slapped her in vexation "you don't understand,,, what I feel for him" he sobbed

"So you sent me those black roses?"

"Yes" he grinned.

"And you tried to kill me in truck?"

"I followed you everywhere. I saw you in circus and I knew I have to take you off that moment, but you were lucky,,, you escaped,,, not this time" he sharpened his knife faster.

"You are a psychopath! Think of those people who could be alive,,, but Shyam has killed many"

"Stop your nonsense. Your time has ended,,, close your eyes" he laughed hysterically. He raised his arm to stab,,

Nynisha screeched "no,,,,,," and closed her eyes.

Suddenly he fell with a thud on the sand and lay unconscious.

Nynisha opened her eyes in surprise. She couldn't believe that she was still alive.

Tom smote the stranger on his head with a rod.

"Tom?,,,, I don't understand,,, you land up like messiah everywhere" she said incredulously.

Tom freed her by removing the knots. Nynisha hugged him in gratitude.

"I don't have words to say,,, if you weren't here,,, I would have been dead!,,,," she sobbed.

"Don't cry,,, get some help,, I will take care of him till you come back"

"But,,,, how can I leave you,,,, he is a psychopath" she was unconvinced.

"I can take care,,,, go,,, hurry,,' he ordered.

Nynisha ran towards the hotel, screaming for help. Siddanth was baffled to see Nynisha and quickly approached her.

Nynisha was panting for breath. Siddanth hugged her and then asked "what happened?"

"He tried to kill me" she pointed towards the shore.

Siddanth turned around "whom? Where?"

"We need more help. He is a psychopath" Nynisha called for the security men. Siddanth stood unable to believe what was going on. "I will explain you on the way, we need to go,,, now!" she pulled his hand and took him towards the beach.

They arrived at the spot, but what waited them was something unexpected.

There was nobody in sight. The place was deserted.

Nynisha ran across in dismay. She searched everywhere "he was here,,,, I was here,,, tied up to this coconut tree,,,, he was about to stab me,,, but Tom saved me,,," she spoke hysterically.

The guards gave a quick look "there is no one here Madam"

"Believe me,,,, he was here,,," she hugged Siddanth and sobbed.

Nynisha was still panicking "where did they disappear? What happened to Tom?"

Siddanth consoled her "let's go to the room"

He made her sit comfortably "relax,, tell me in detail" he said. Nynisha revealed the horrible ordeal she had just undergone.

"Let's inform the police and we will leave" he pacified her.

They reached the airport and waited in the lounge. The local news channel was telecasted.

"Indian man found dead in beach"

"Siddanth,, look at the television, isn't he our minister son?" Nynisha pointed at the screen.

"Yes,, he is" Siddanth looked on in shock.

The honeymoon had ended in a mystery. Too many incidents anguished her. "What's happening?" her mind was tormented with questions.

Chapter 19

Nynisha and Siddanth arrived home. 'Welcome back sweethearts!" Lakshmi hugged them.

"How was the honeymoon? You look tired after all those workouts" she teased. "I am waiting to see your snaps, hope they are censored!" she patted him.

Nynisha gave a faint smile. Siddanth eyed her and she knew what he meant 'keep quiet, don't reveal'

"It was real fun, we truly enjoyed" Nynisha hugged Lakshmi.

"take rest,,, I have lots of things to gossip on,,,' Laksmi told Nynisha.

Nynisha sat on her couch and her mind brooded with thoughts. "Enough of mulling over, let me do some work" she unpacked her bags and took out the clothes for laundry.

Something caught her eye. A coat was hung at the corner of the room. She went near and pulled out the coat. "This is Tom s coat" then she remembered how he had saved her at the river and how they had shared nostalgic school memories

"My messiah" she grinned. "Where did you disappear?"
A diary popped out of a pocket. She opened it to read

To sin is to invite misery
And for that invitation
I am glad to redeem
What you deserve
For the pain you have caused me
I pledge to destroy you all
One by one.......
,,,,,,,,, one by one

Nynisha was puzzled to read the first page. Her fingers flipped opened the second page.

It was a sketch of a man falling off a cliff. Underneath it was written

Sijas,,, meet your maker with a split skull

"Nice sketch",,, she thought,, "he has an art. But,, I don't understand"

She flipped the next page. It was another drawing of a man with a rod in his anus

Underneath it was written,,,

Sulaiman,,,,, sodomized to death

She was baffled to see the image. It was truly surreal. "Why has he drawn such images? I can't imagine him having such criminal thoughts. He was such a nice boy in school days. Is this a joke? A fiction? A story? She thought

She flipped the next page

It was drawing of a man struggling for oxygen in scuba diving

Underneath it was written

Jayanth,,, struggled for air

It can't be,,, he must have written a fictional story she thought,,, may be his ideas of a story. He is timid,, he can't kill,,

She turned the next page

It was a drawing of man lying on a beach

Underneath it was written

Sahil,,, intoxicated to death

"Sahil? The name sounds familiar. Who is Sahil?" then suddenly she remembered the television news in airport. "Sahil,, the minister son found dead in beach!"

Nynisha dropped the diary in horror. Then it dawned on her.

"Tom killed him!,,, Tom killed all of these!,, no,,,,,, she screeched,,,,, he is my messiah,, he has saved me twice,,, he can't kill,,, it's impossible,," she clutched her head in pain.

She sank on the floor and the diary had opened its last page

It was drawing of a man getting beheaded.

Underneath it was written

Mike,,, beheaded

Her lips trembled and tears welled up her eyes. She felt dizzy.

"Why did you kill them?,,,,," A shiver ran down her spine.

Nynisha sat frozen when her cell phone rang. It was her boss.

"Good morning Nynisha. I hope you had a great holiday. I have some project to assign you. I am sick and I wouldn't be able to visit office. Come home and pick up the papers" George said.

Nynisha came back to her senses 'sure sir, I am coming"

She placed the phone down and looked at the diary again. "I need to inform the police" she thought.

She quickly packed her bags took along the diary and hurried towards George house.

She reached the house and knocked the door. A servant opened.

"I am Nynisha, boss had called" Nynisha spoke to the servant.

The servant replied "he is ill on bed. You can meet him upstairs in his room"

'Poor George' she thought. She traipsed the stairs and went to his room.

George was sleeping on the bed. Nynisha didn't want to wake up the old man. "Let me search for papers,, it must be somewhere here" she thought. She walked across the room and looked around.

The room was wonderfully decorated with antique pieces. The books and papers were in neat order. A man of opulence, she thought and why not,,, he was the owner of a top leading magazine in the state.

A family photo caught her attention. A happy family photo of three, George, his wife and his son. She looked on for some time. Her son looked familiar to her. He was smart and handsome with a modern hairstyle. Suddenly it dawned to her,, he was none other but Tom.

"Tom!,,, George s son! Unbelievable,,," Nynisha was baffled.

She ran out of the room in perspiration. The servant looked on, but she quickly moved out.

Fears and concerns paled in, she felt dizzy. The layers were opening up,, one by one,,

She didn't know what to do and where to go. Her instincts moved her to police station.

She barged into the inspector s cabin. The officer was startled for a second.

"good afternoon Nynisha,, so did you meet your killer?' the police officer grinned.

Nynisha slowly revealed the incidents that had occurred in island and how Tom had saved her. She also revealed,, how baffled was she to see them disappear.

"It sounds interesting" he stuttered

"It doesn't end with that,,, New things have cropped up" she frowned.

"and what are they?' he cocked his brow

"I know who killed Sahil"

"Sahil?"

"That minister son who was found dead in island"

"That's great!" the inspector dreamt of how he could boast in front of media that he had solved the case.

"So who is the killer?"

"Tom" she said hesitantly.

"Tom?"

"Tom is the son of verity magazine owner George Patrick" she fumbled.

"The media will love this!" He thought

"What makes you say so,,, do you have any evidence?"

Nynisha handed the diary to him. The inspector quickly flipped opened the pages and was disappointed. He threw the diary back on the table.

'This is useless" he snapped. "We cannot just arrest him because of this stupid diary. He can easily quote this as an alibi. He may say that this is his fictional story."

"My sixth sense say,,, all these murders are true" Nynisha said imperiously.

"Mrs. Nynisha,,, police cannot rely on your sixth sense" he said gruffly

Nynisha resented "it is not just a single murder, but a series,, look at those pictures,, each one killed in different manner. You can just check in your data bases. Tom has mentioned the names of victims too,,, Sijas, Sulaiman, Jayanth, Sahil and Mike. You can check for them"

"Ok,,, leave the diary with us,, we will try" he gabbled.

Nynisha walked out tormented.

Chapter 20

TOM SAT ON CHAIR AND wriggled. His every neuron was firing in anger.

I am losing patience,,, kill him fast,, the last one,,, mike

Tom heard his master's voice. 'I will master' he said. His left hand slapped him. He looked at it furiously 'I will chop you off, once my work is done' he scowled

Tom dialed his cell phone 'did you find Mike?

"Yes, he is working as pimp. You can find him in Red Street' someone answered.

"Good! You will receive your money" Tom cut the call.

Mike enjoyed his work as a pimp and what else a bastard could work as. He was completely involved in women trafficking and enjoyed his nights in brothels. He was lucky enough to escape police raids.

Tom arrived at the Red street. The prostitutes were alluring him with their flaunting bodies. He was least interested in them. His only aim was,,,,,,, finding Mike.

One last soul to be taken

"Do you want any help? I can get you wonderful offers" a stranger stopped him. Tom looked at him malevolently and pushed him away.

"Wait! I can get you the basic offer. Only five hundred rupees for one hour" he smiled as he said that.

Tom banged his face and yelled "get lost"

The stranger was frightened and began to run. "Wait!" Tom called him back. The stranger turned around in surprise.

"I have something to offer" Tom said as he took out a bunch of notes.

The stranger was frenzied seeing money, he tried snatching them. "Wait! Not so easy!,,," Tom showed a photo of Mike "where can I find him?" he asked.

The stranger looked at the photo and was alarmed. "You police? He muttered and began to run.

Tom hurried behind him. The chase was faster as the stranger made quick turns, in small passages and Tom was losing him.

Tom ran as fast as he could and finally caught him.

Tom smote him on his face. "I am not a police. Don't run. I am his old friend and have some old debts to deal with."

The stranger smirked, "not police?"

"Yes, I am his old friend. Want to meet him. Where can I find him?"

"He is not here. Out of station."

"Don't lie" Tom barked in anger.

"True,,,,,, He will be returning next week with new set of women."

"That's good" Tom offered him a bunch of notes 'call me,,, when he is back"

The stranger was happy with money "sure,," he smiled.

Tom left in the dark shades of the passages.

Tom was getting impatient. One week seemed longer. His frustration, vengeance grew day by day.

The cell phone rang. It was the stranger.

"Mike is back" he said.

"Good! I am coming" Tom grinned.

He floored on the accelerator and his car took off with a bang. He was waiting for that moment.

Tom was caught up in traffic and his irritation made him neurotic. He had stopped his car at a signal when Nynisha suddenly noticed him.

"Tom!,,,,,,, unbelievable" she was excited to see him. She needed answers to all her questions and only Tom could answer them. The mystery of the diary has to be solved she thought.

Tom hurried as the signal turned green. Nynisha didn't want to miss this chance and she quickly followed him.

Tom was entering the Red street.

"Why the hell, is he visiting Red Street? Now,,, he want woman?" she was intrigued.

Tom parked his car and entered an old building. Nynisha hated to enter. She could be caught by some goons. She could be mistaken for a prostitute. She covered her face with a shawl and scurried behind him.

Mike was alone in a room and he was smoking a cigar.

Tom knocked the door. "Come in" Mike said.

"My assistant said,, you would be coming. Your face looks familiar,,, who are you?" Mike looked at him.

Nynisha hid herself in a corner to listen to the conversation.

"Hello Mike,,, nice to see you after long time, Tom smiled.

Nynisha was startled. "Mike? He is the last victim in that diary,,, my sixth sense was true,, Tom has murdered all those victims,,,, but why?" she thought.

"We are acquaintances,,, we studied in same college" Tom spoke.

Mike grinned "may be,,,, now what do you want? Woman?"

Tom s face flushed and his eyes turned red in anger. "Can't you think of anything else in this world?" he opened a box and took out a sword.

Mike looked at him alarmed "what the hell?"

Tom plunged on him with a sword. Mike defended himself with a pillow. They fought like enemies on the ground.

Mike caught an iron box and threw at him. It stuck Tom on the head and he fell unconscious.

Mike laughed sardonically "I took you off in a second,,, poor guy" he took his sword and was about to strike Tom when he was alarmed by a police siren.

He quickly dropped the sword and escaped.

Nynisha looked on in horror and then came to her senses. She reached at Tom and sprinkled some water. Tom was hurt and he couldn't get up.

Nynisha instantly called an ambulance and informed the police.

Chapter 21

TOM GAINED CONSCIOUS AND LOOKED around. Nynisha was sitting next to him.

"Relax Tom,,, you are in hospital" she smirked.

"Hospital?" he then remembered how he was stuck by an iron box.

"Nynisha? I don't understand? Why are you here?" he asked

"A long story" she said.

A police officer intervened "hello Tom,, you need to answer some questions"

"Why were you killing Mike?

"No,, I didn't"

"Do not lie" Nynisha has a recorded video of your fight.

Tom looked at Nynisha "I can't tell" he said flatly.

The officer placed a diary on his lap. "Is this yours?'

Tom looked at the diary in surprise "how did you get this?" he asked the officer.

The officer cocked his brow "how we got the diary is not important. What made you write this diary? And why have you murdered these people?"

"No,,,,, I haven't murdered" he yelled.

"We have searched in our database. Sijas was found with a split skull under a cliff. The local villagers had notified. Sulaiman had escaped from a jail, later he was found sodomized to death in a mountain. Andaman police confirmed that Jayanth never returned from scuba diving. Sahil was found intoxicated to death in another country,,, and now,,, last but,, not the least,,,, you tried killing Mike!

Everything has happened as you have described in the diary,, you cannot escape,,, we need answers,, now!" the officer spoke ferociously.

Tom clutched his head and yelled. He then laughed hysterically. The next moment he cried jabbing his head. He had become neurotic and was uncontrollable.

Nynisha looked at the officer "you can interrogate him,,, later" she swiftly called the doctors.

Dr Siddanth arrived and took control of the situation.

"Relax Tom,,,, I can help you" he reassured him.

"Leave me alone!" Tom screeched.

"Okay,,, call me if you want help" Siddanth left the room

Siddanth met the police officer "we will keep him in observation. He needs time. He is broken down"

Tom lamented, screeched and yelled. He laughed at his destiny. He heard his master s voice

Stop it,,,,,,, it's not over,,,,,, one more soul to be taken,,,,,, you cannot sit here and cry,,, you need to act,, you need to escape

Tom was conversing with his master. He planned with him how to escape.

His left hand was fidgeting. It slapped him, removed his shirt. It had become uncontrollable.

Siddanth observed his behavior in a computer. Toms every act was monitored.

The police officer looked on startled. "With whom is he talking to? Why is he slapping himself? What's wrong with him?

Siddanth looked on and said "I think he is hallucinating. The way he is speaking to somebody clearly says so. I need to talk to him"

"Do you mean to say,,, he is psychotic? Or is he feigning to escape trial?" the officer looked at him suspiciously

"Unless I speak to him,, I cannot say,, give me time"

"Sure,, keep us updated" I will make a move

Siddanth observed Tom for some time and approached him.

"Hello Tom,, how are you feeling,, do you need any help?"

"I don't need your help,, just let me go" Tom scowled.

"Relax Tom,,, I saw you talking to someone,, may I ask who is it?"

"It's none of your business!" Tom snapped

"Come on Tom,,, I assure you no harm,, I am a doctor,, I can help,, so,, who is it? Is he your friend?"

"Not friend,,, he is my master" Tom said.

"Ok,, so what does your master say? Can you see him now?"

"No,, I can only hear him. He is my godfather,, he just commands,, I am obliged to obey him"

"Since when are you hearing from your master?"

"No idea"

"And why were you slapping yourself?"

"It's not me,, it's my left hand,, it doesn't obey me,, its possessed by some evil"

"Tom you were admitted in this hospital before. Do you remember?"

"Yes,, I had some head problem"

"Good,, you remember,, Dr Philip had treated you. Something special had happened. You had slapped a nurse and had squeezed her breast"

"it was unintentional,, I still feel sorry for that nurse,, I told you,, it's my left hand,, its evil" Tom blabbered.

"Ok,,, so what all your left hand does? And since when is it behaving abnormal?"

"Its acting weird since I came to this hospital,, It was fine before"

"You had head injury right,, you were collided with a car?"

"Yes"

"Then,, what else does it do?"

"It unbuttons my shirt,, it slaps me,, it exchanges my shoes,, it's totally freaky" Tom went on

"I saw your diary, the drawings are scary,,, so is it true?"

Tom remained silent

"I can help you Tom,, do tell"

Tom clutched his head and screamed "enough,,, leave me alone"

Siddanth didn't was to pressurize him. "Relax tom,, will see you tomorrow"

Nynisha was waiting outside. "What happened? Did you find out something?"

"I need to study this case, give me time" Siddanth swiftly went to his cabin and opened up his medical books. He searched the web and then it dawned on him

The police officer was waiting to meet Siddanth.

"Anything new cropped up?" the officer asked

"Yes,, Tom has hallucinations and Alien hand syndrome"

"What?" the officer looked at him totally puzzled

"He is suffering from a rare neurological disorder called Alien hand syndrome in which one hand functions involuntarily, with the victim completely unaware of its action."

"Its freaky!" the officer was surprised

"It may sound so,, but its science"

"Ok,, what about those murders? Did he kill them because of his illness? Or did he really have some motive?"

"He didn't open up,, I will try today, I have to open up layers one by one,, I cannot hurry"

"Thanks doc,, I am waiting"

Nynisha waited for Siddanth "can I talk to Tom? Please,,,"

"He is paranoiac,, he may be harmful" Siddanth was worried.

"He has saved me twice,, he won't harm me,,, I need answers,,, please…"

Siddanth agreed hesitantly.

Tom was looking across window when Nynisha entered. "Hello Tom,, how are you"

Tom looked at her and smirked "I was expecting you,," he said

"I remember you as an innocent boy,,, you were my messiah,,,,, I am unable to believe,,, what's happening?,, where did you disappear in that island? And,, what is all about this diary,, why are you doing it,, Tom,, please,, tell me" Nynisha caressed his hand in a friendly way.

"You are one of the persons whom I will always remember,, you had come like an angel,,, when I didn't had any friends in school,, you had become my best friend,, but,, you left me alone,,,"

"I was a kid tom,,, I had to go with my parents,," her eyes were moist

"I was vexed when that stranger wanted to kill you,,, I couldn't take it,,, he was killing an innocent woman,,, he was killing my child hood friend,, I was aghast,, he deserved death,, so I drowned him in that sea.." he said flatly

Nynisha sat frozen; she couldn't believe what he just uttered. "Why did you kill him? I was getting help,, I was getting police"

"It's over,, Nynisha,,, now,,, you are free,,, live your life,," he smiled

"I can't understand you Tom,,, why are you doing all these?,,, please tell,, I can help you out,,,"

"I don't need any help,,, Nynisha,,, and,, no one can stop me,,,"

"What do you mean?"

"Mike is still alive,,,,"

"No,,, you can't do that,, you have already killed many…" she said fearing

"No one can stop me,,, no one,,, no one,,," he laughed hysterically

Nynisha ran out in fear. "Siddanth,,, he is paranoiac,,, he said,, he is going to kill Mike,,"

"What?" Siddanth was baffled

Nynisha swiftly informed the police. Tom s security was tightened.

Nynisha couldn't sleep in the night. Nightmares tormented her. She saw Tom beheading mike.

"No,,," she awoke in perspiration. "Why is he doing it? There must be a reason,, what?" she pondered

It was early morning and windy breeze, billowed her hair. She had not slept. She stood in balcony witnessing the rain. Lightning and thunder roared in the sky

What was it indicating? She looked on perturbed.

Suddenly she heard her cell phone ringing. She picked up "Tom has escaped" a police officer said. Nynisha dropped her phone in shock

She turned towards the window. Nature was in fury and so was Tom. What awaited her was unbelievable.

Chapter 22

THE POLICE WAS QUICK ON alert. All the city perimeters were blocked. A police team was sent to George house.

George was suddenly disturbed by the police siren. He peeped into the window. Police vehicles and officers had surrounded his house.

"What the hell?" he traipsed down the stairs faster.

"Good morning Mr. George, we have a search warrant" an officer gave him a paper.

"Search warrant,, for what?" he looked questionably

"In search of Tom,, your son"

"Tom!" George couldn't believe his ears. "Why are you searching him? What has he done?'

"Your son has murdered four people and now he is on way to murder Mike"

"Murder!,,, Tom?,,, no way,.,, impossible!" George howled.

"I request you to cooperate" the police searched his entire house

"Officer,, I need to know,, what's happening?"

"You can meet Dr Siddanth,, he has something more to say about your son"

The police constables searched the entire house. They didn't find Tom.

"Please inform us,, if he arrives here" the officer told George and left.

George was disturbed and withered. He decided to meet Dr Siddanth and he reached hospital.

"Police is in search of Tom,,, the officer said you have something more to say,, I am concerned"

"Before I say what has happened,, I want you to see a footage" Siddanth took him to a cabin. George sat in horror as he saw his son behaving like a mad man. His screeching, lamenting and slapping himself,, everything was weird.

"Your son is neurotic, he has hallucinations,, he says his master advice him to kill,, he says his hands is freaky,, controlled by an evil. He has a rare disorder called Alien hand syndrome.

George looked on petrified.

This is Tom s diary,, have a look" Dr Siddanth said

George flipped opened the pages. The drawings, their depiction was nothing less than a horror story.

"Every drawing in this diary has become an incident. Tom has murdered all of them,, now he has escaped in search of Mike,, his last target is still alive.

"What's wrong with my son,, he was so fine,,, what has happened to him,, I can't imagine him as a murderer,, why is he doing it,, has he become psychotic?

"The cause for these murders is still not known,, only Tom can explain.. Or he may be doing these because he is ill. Homicidal tendencies are common in schizophrenia

George felt tightness in throat and heaviness in heart. He sank and cringed.

Siddanth pitied him. "Do you need help?" he placed his hand on his shoulder

"No thanks,," George slowly walked out without talking a word. Pain and agony made him wither. He remembered Tom as a small boy. Tom was innocent and timid and was lovable as a child.

"What made him evil? What caused him?" George wanted to hug Tom and ask. "Where are you my son?" he cried.

George stepped out of hospital and media persons charged him with questions "what do you want to say about your son? Was he psychotic since childhood? Did he kill people because of psychosis? Or he is feigning to be a psychotic? Why did he kill all of them? What did minister son Sahil do to him? Why did he kill him?"

George was taken back with questions, he yelled at them "please stop it,,, leave me alone,,"

He hurried towards his car and quickly drove off.

He reached home perturbed. Grief had striped his heart into thousand pieces and he felt as bereaved soul.

"What have you done…" he looked at Tom s photo. "Didn't I play my role as a father well? Didn't I give you whatever you had asked for? Did I fail you? Or was it my mistake? Didn't I give you time? What kind of a father am I? Why couldn't I see,, what was happening to you? Was I so busy? You were so innocent and timid and a lovely child,, when did you turn into evil? When…" George sobbed sinking on the floor.

He slowly pulled a drawer and searched. He picked up a revolver. He faced Tom's photo for one last time. Tom was smiling,,, George placed it at his forehead and triggered.

He fell dead instantly.

Chapter 23

TOM WANDERED RELENTLESSLY. TIME WAS running out. His eyes had become weary and his muscles had become weak. He perched on a stone and breathed a heavy sigh in desperation.

You ought to be running,,,, you can't take rest,,, get up,, his master was growling

"Yes master,, everything has to end today" he said. But,,, where to find Mike? It was a big question. Tom knew Mike won't be wandering with his ladies in Red Street. Police were searching him too.

"help me god,,, help me,,, you have to,, you know what that bastard has done,,, he can't be alive any longer,, his sins are growing beyond limitations,,, it has to end" Tom was lost in thoughts.

He was losing hope. "What if the police find me? What if I die before I fulfill my last task? I need to hurry,,, I have to find Mike soon"

He covered himself in a shawl and wandered in a market. His eyes searched for only one face,, Mike.

Suddenly he stumbled upon someone. To his surprise, he was the same stranger,,, an assistant of Mike.

The stranger was startled to see Tom and his instincts made him run. Tom chased him like a leopard,,,, yelling at him "wait,, don't run,,,"

Tom struggled and was able to grab his shirt. The stranger fell and faced Tom.

"Where is Mike?" Tom snapped

"I don't know" he muttered

Tom smote him on his face "you have no idea,,, how dangerous I am,,, so,,, just bark!" Tom scowled.

The stranger frightened at his vicious stare "Mike is hiding in an old mansion"

Tom grinned sinisterly and said "thanks"

He hurried towards the mansion.

The old dilapidated mansion looked scary with creepy cobwebs and pigeons haunting around. The door was locked. He searched for an entry. Crumbling window panes gave him way. He slowly slid across and fell inside.

Tom was cautious in his every step. He knew he should not alert Mike. He looked around in the big mansion. Old artifacts and portraits were hung and were loaded with dust. He searched the rooms and then he saw smoke emitting from attic.

He smelled cigar. Tom looked up "you are hiding there,,," he smirked. He traipsed the stairs slowly without making noise and reached the attic.

Mike was busy with a cigar, lost in his own thoughts. Tom slowly neared him and placed the edge of the sword on his neck.

Tom had acquired a sword as he traipsed the stairs. It was hung among the antiques.

Mike squirmed in his chair and looked on in raw terror.

Tom gave him a cold look "wondering how I reached here?" he laughed sinisterly, "god sent me,,, your sins have grown beyond limitations,, it has to end"

"But,, why do you want to kill me? What have I done to you?" Mike muttered

"Do you remember Anne Fernandez?" Tom said scornfully

Mike pondered a moment and quickly realized why Tom was behind him. He swiftly scuttled towards the door. The door was locked. He perspired and hurried towards the window and looked down. Rocks were beckoning him to death.

Tom laughed hysterically "there is no way,, you can escape" then in a fraction of second, he plunged on him.

Mike decided to fight and he laid his defense. Mike hit on Tom s leg, making him lose his balance. The sword flew in the air and Mike caught it.

Mike laughed at him "it's my turn" he plunged on him to strike.

Tom escaped and he quickly looked around. He found chains and he acquired it as fast as he could. He lashed them on Mike and the sword fell off from his hand.

Tom smashed him with chains and quickly manacled him. He dragged him towards a table and made his head lie on the edge.

"My drawing has to come true,, I had decided to behead you,,, and so you will,," Tom lifted his hand in trajectory and gave one last stroke beheading Mike.

Blood splashed on Tom s face and he wiped it in vengeance.

Tom dropped the sword and looked for a last time at the monster.

He walked out of mansion. The rain drops fell, washing away the blood on his body. He felt clean and happy.

Everything was over. He had accomplished what he set out for. The misery, the grief, the agony, all had striped his heart into thousand pieces.

He walked and walked and there was nothing more left. He perched on a rock and a thorn pricked him. He pulled out the thorn and he saw a rose peeping in a bush. He plucked and looked at his beauty.

Tom slowly descended down in a cemetery and searched for a tomb. And,,, it caught his eye,,, Anne Fernandez. He perched beside in desperation and laid the rose on top of it. He looked longingly at the name and tears weld up his eyes. He rested his head on the grave and his emotions burst opened. He cried. But the rain drops washed it making him look feebler.

He was filled with nostalgia as he remembered her. Her laughter and her warmth had given him a new meaning. He cried at the thought of never seeing her again.

"I miss you" he said and he hugged the stone.

He slowly got up to walk. He muscles ached but he had to keep moving. He walked till he saw a church.

He smiled "Lord,,, I am coming" he said.

He entered the church and prayed for one last time. Then he walked to a clock tower. He looked up to see the time. It was ten minutes before twelve. Ten minutes and he would be entering into his twenty third year. It was his birthday.

Ten minutes more,,, he thought. He walked inside and began to climb the stairs to reach the top.

As he reached the top he witnessed the large clock with iron frame. The dials ticked and he felt his time was nearing.

He reached the top and slid across the window. Now, he was facing the world he was born.

Memories swift past him like a time travel. He saw himself as a child carried by his mother. His father played with him and made him happy. He then remembered Nynisha,, his school friend.

He then saw Anne. He thought of those beautiful memories.

He remembered all the happiness that life had once offered him.

But it didn't last long. Cruel memories tried to pop up, but he quickly surpassed it.

He looked at the sky. It was lightning and the clouds roared in their thunder. He felt the nature was with him.

The clock struck twelve and it was time for him to end. He didn't know what to call,,,, his birthday or his death day.

Tom opened up his arms and looked towards the sky "I don't want mercy,, my lord,, from dust I came and to dust I will return"

He fell, facing to the ground along with the rain drops cutting through his skin. He saw flashes of memories one by one, as gravity pulled him down, closer to death.

He saw the face of Anne for one last time before he hit the ground. He could feel life stripping apart him, as his bones broke to thousand pieces and blood oozed from the bruises.

He died in an instant.

Chapter 24

TWO DAYS HAD PASSED AND the relentless rain had stopped. It was bright and sunny. Nynisha walked with a wreath of flowers. She was in a cemetery and she searched for a grave stone.

Then she saw two grave stones next to each other like father and son. It was of George Patrick and Tom Patrick. Both had the same inscription.

Rest in peace

Nynisha placed the wreath on Tom s grave. She looked at the stone longingly. Her mind was still tormented with questions.

Who would answer them? She had no idea.

Suddenly she felt someone brushing her back. It was Siddanth. "I knew you would be here. I have something to show you" he placed an envelope in her hand

"What's it?" she asked

"A letter,,, which I found today morning. It was hidden among other envelopes on my table"

Nynisha looked at him "I don't understand" she said.

"Open" he said

Her heart panicked as she read that letter.

Dear Nynisha,

I won't be alive when you are reading this letter. I cherished you in my memories as a best friend. I will always remember you as a beautiful angel.

I am sure,, you will come to my grave seeking answers,,, and I won't disappoint you.

Life is unpredictable and uncertain. What you wish doesn't happen,,, and what happens,, you wouldn't have wished for,,,,

Here,,,,,, I say you,,, my untold story,,,

I was innocent as a child,,, I played in my own dream world,, and,, I liked solitude.

You came along as an angel,,, and in you,,,,,,,,,, I found a good friend.

But,, life plays its own game,,, you left me alone,,,, I was heartbroken,,, and I had lost a good friend.

It was then I witnessed my first horror,,, Sulaiman had entered. He was appointed as a new driver. He was horrific and I still remember his malicious eyes.

I was scared as a child. He sodomized me,,,,,, and it was unbearable.

He threatened me,,, if I ever disclose,,, I would be dead,,

I feared him,,, I couldn't do anything as a child,, except to scream,,

Luckily,, my dad changed my school... I felt free from that demon,,

But,,, no,,, he always haunted me in my dreams,,, I could never sleep... I was hurt and broken,, traumatized and vulnerable,,,

I grew up to face more people,,, but,,, I had become an introvert.

I was scared to talk and I was scared of strangers.

Destiny smiled at me,,, and Anne came into my life. My life was blooming and I had surpassed the darkness. I was out of abyss,, I found love.

The moments with her,,, were of pure happiness. Life handed me adversity.

She was a good painter and her artistic paintings made me love her more. I developed a passion of drawing and sketching. We spent time under the trees, painting and drawing the wonderful nature.

Her warmth and affection made me alive. I was born again,, in a new world,, a world of love and care.

Everything was beautiful,,, everything was nice,,,

Then,,,,,,,,,,, the unfortunate incident occurred.

The students wanted a trekking expedition. Anne was excited about it. but,, my instincts said,,

Something inevitable was coming up.

I was reluctant to go,,, but,, she forced me.

We set out on trekking expedition. It was fun. There were green mountains, narrow dark tunnels, tall bridges.

The group was a mixture of all semesters, and I witnessed an eve teasing by a group. I told Anne,, to keep away from those boys. I wanted to protect her.

We camped in the night. There was dance, music,, fun at camp fire.

It was my birthday and Anne had promised me with a surprise. I was waiting.

A group of boys were drunk and had become uncontrollable. I advised Anne to leave and left for our camp. It was midnight twelve and she surprised me with cakes and candles. I was really happy. I felt blessed. The small party was over and we ended up in sleep.

It was midnight,, and I got up in fear. I was perspiring,, I dint know the cause of my anxiety. I hurried towards Anne s camp, but she was not to be found. I enquired her friends,, they said she went out to fetch water sometime ago,, still not returned.

My heart paced,,, something was wrong. It was dark and I went in search of her. I stumbled upon a rock and my hands caught something,, it was her anklets.

Where is Anne?

I ran inside the forest. It was dark and a faint moon light illuminated the trees and spaces. I ran yelling her name,,, and I stumbled again,, this time,, it was not a rock,,, it was Anne,,,

I had stumbled upon Anne,, and when I looked,,, I froze.

She was savagely attacked and brutally raped. She was bleeding to death.

I cringed at her body and I was numb. I held her and tears welled up my eyes. She was breathing fast. Her last few words striped my heart

"Don't leave those bastards,,, kill them,,,, I don't want any other girl to face the same ordeal,, they are treat,, promise me,,, kill them,,"

"Who Anne?" I sobbed

"Sijas,,,,, Jayanth,,,, Sahil,,,,, Mike" she struggled to utter those names.

Her lungs were rattling and she was struggling to breathe,, and,,, she spoke for a last time,,

"I love you"

Then,,,,,,,, she was dead.

I embraced her and shrieked,,, I cried,,, I yelled,, I lamented.

It was then,, my retribution had begun,,, I had pledged,, to kill,, one by one,,

They deserved death and nothing else.

A last goodbye

Tom Patrick

Epilogue

WHEN SOMETHING GOES WRONG, EMOTIONS are hurt. How can the world be so unfair?

But, we still wake up every morning with a hope and faith that things will be better.

Why Pranav hated women? Was it because of his past? Why was he madly in love with Prisha? Why he developed a deadly passion?

Why did the stranger wanted to kill Nynisha? Why couldn't he see what his lover Shyam had done? Can love take us to such extremes?

Can a man like Sulaiman be tolerated? He was sodomizing children. He had raped his own daughter. Why was he such a monster?

Sijas, Jayanth, Sahil and Mike had raped a girl brutally. She ended up in death.

Should these people left free? Such animal behavior is intolerable

Tom was livid with the world around him. He was heartbroken, depressed and he was afflicted. The inhumanity was miserable. His mind was tormented and he was mentally ill. He behaved savagely, but why?

What was his fault? Why did he face what he never deserved?

Was it his illness? Or the people around him made him evil?

Who is mad after all?

Printed in the United States
By Bookmasters